The
Unwilling
Witch

The Unwilling Witch

A MONSTERRIFIC TALE

DAVID LUBAR

STARSCAPE

A Tom Doherty Associates Book
New York

THE UNWILLING WITCH

Copyright © 1997 by David Lubar

The Wavering Werewolf excerpt copyright © 1997 by David Lubar

Illustrations by Marcos Calo

A Starscape Book
Published by Tom Doherty Associates, LLC
175 Fifth Avenue
New York, NY 10010

www.tor-forge.com

The Library of Congress Cataloging-in-Publication Data
is available upon request.

ISBN 978-0-7653-3078-9 (hardcover)
ISBN 978-1-4299-9309-8 (e-book)

Starscape books may be purchased for educational, business, or promotional use. For information on bulk purchases, please contact Macmillan Corporate and Premium Sales Department at 1-800-221-7945, extension 5442, or write specialmarkets@macmillan.com.

First Edition: September 2013

Printed in the United States of America

0 9 8 7 6 5 4 3 2 1

For Alison,
who scares me sometimes

Contents

Author's Note

I've always been a fan of monsters. As a kid, I watched monster movies, read monster magazines, built monster models, and even tried my hand at monster makeup for Halloween. Basically, I was a creepy little kid. It's no surprise that, when I grew up and became a writer, I would tell monster stories. I've written a lot of them over the years. My short-story collections, such as *Attack of the Vampire Weenies and Other Warped and Creepy Tales*, are full of vampires, werewolves, ghosts, witches, giant insects, and other classic creatures. The book you hold in your hands is also about a monster. But it is different from my short stories in a wonderful way. Let me explain.

Years ago, I decided I wanted to tell a tale through the eyes of a monster. That idea excited me, but it didn't feel special enough, by itself. Then I had a second idea that went perfectly with the first one. What if a kid became a monster? Even better—what if the kid had to decide whether to remain as a monster, or to become human again? The result of these ideas was not one book, but six. It seems the town of Lewington attracts a monster-riffic amount of trouble. To find out more, read on.

The Unwilling Witch

One

OLD LADY WHO?

I almost walked right past the woman.

She was huddled on a bench, so quiet that I didn't pay any attention to her at first. But her trembling caught my eye. She was scrunched up and shaking all over. I was on my way to meet my friend Jan at the edge of the park across from the mall. Usually, I got there first. This time, Jan would have to wait.

"Are you all right?" I moved closer, hoping I could figure out what was wrong.

She didn't answer me.

"Ma'am, are you okay? Do you need some help?"

She raised her head.

I saw a doll once with a face made from a dried apple—all deep, dark wrinkles and hard ridges. That was her, but she looked even older than that doll. Her eyes stared past me into the distance.

I tried to get her attention. "Should I go for help?" I reached out to touch her shoulder and let her know I wasn't running away. "I'm coming back. Don't worry—I'll bring someone who can help. You'll be fine."

Her right hand shot out and clutched my wrist. It was so quick and unexpected, I shrieked in surprise.

"No time," she whispered.

"There's time," I told her. "There's always time. Let me get help."

"The moment for passing is here." She searched the park with her eyes as she spoke. "It must be now. Now or never. Now or lost forever."

I tried to step back. I didn't want to hurt her, but I had to break loose. I expected to slip easily from her withered fingers, but they held me like her hand was a steel claw. "It's okay. I can get help. Just let me go. Please." I tried to stay calm, but I hated the feeling of being trapped.

Her grip tightened. She pulled me closer, then raised her left hand toward my face. "Mine is done," she said, slowly and clearly. "Yours has begun."

As she touched me, a blast of power surged through my forehead. It was like walking in front of a giant water hose. The force washed over me with so much strength that I was thrown free of her grip. I hit the ground hard. I looked up, expecting her to be tossed over the back of the bench. I winced at the thought of those old, brittle bones breaking. But she was on her feet.

"Wait!" I couldn't let her move.

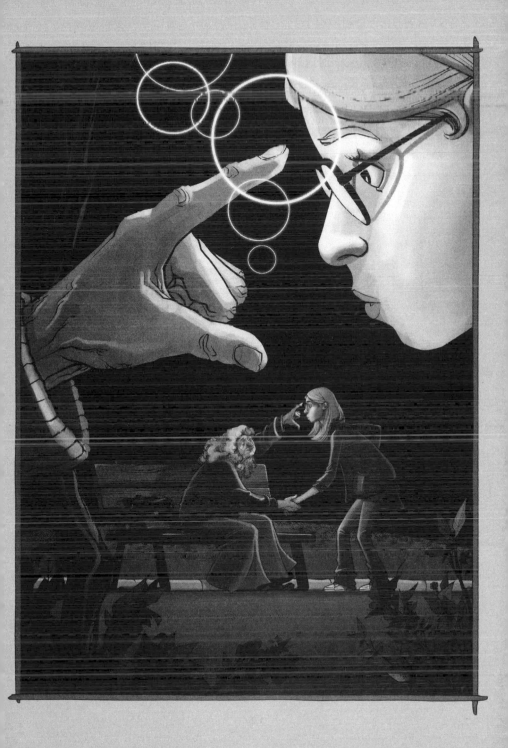

She faced me for a moment. "Wisdom and kindness," she said. Then she sped away. The helpless, shivering woman fled down the path, fast as a young girl, gaining speed with each step, her black dress flapping behind her in the breeze like a flock of ravens.

Two

WITCH WAY?

She disappeared around a bend in the path. In my last glimpse of her, she thrust her arms out to the sides. Her feet seemed to skim the ground. As crazy as this might sound, she made me think of someone trying to launch a kite. I staggered to my feet, then chased after her. She couldn't have gotten far. I rushed past the bushes that were between us.

She was gone.

All I saw was a bird. A large black bird was taking flight. I watched as it pulled itself higher with each wing thrust. The bird became a small dark shape. Then the dark shape became a dot. As the dot vanished, I saw a flash of dazzling white light against the blue sky.

I stared up at the emptiness for a moment, then stumbled back to the bench. My wrist was sore where she'd grabbed me. The skin felt hot. My forehead felt hot, too. I tried to figure out what had happened. She'd muttered words about "passing," but none of it made sense.

"Angie, are you okay?"

I looked up and saw Jan trotting down the path from the direction of the mall.

"I'm fine," I called.

As she got closer, I noticed she was carrying a sign printed on a piece of poster board: SAVE THE WHALES FOR THE CHILDREN. Jan's parents were always rescuing animals or saving trees or fighting for other good causes. Jan helped them out by putting up posters.

"What were you doing?" she asked.

"Just resting." It felt funny telling her that, because it wasn't the whole truth. But I wasn't sure what the truth was. As I looked away, avoiding her eyes, I spotted a mistake on the second line of the poster. It said: WE ARE THERE ONLY HOPE. Jan's parents are scientists. I guess they spent so much time studying really deep things like physics and chemistry that they never learned to spell.

"Hey, that's wrong," I said.

"Where?" she asked. At least in this way, Jan is just like her parents. She's such a bad speller, it's a lucky thing she has a three-letter name.

I pointed to the second line. "There." As I touched it, I felt a tiny shock. I jerked my finger away and looked at the line again: WE ARE THEIR ONLY HOPE. I could have sworn . . .

"Where?" Jan asked again.

18

"My mistake. Let's get going." I still felt a little dizzy. Maybe that explained why I'd misread the sign. Just to make sure nothing strange was going on, I touched another word on the poster. No shock. Everything seemed normal. That was good—I liked normal.

"Sorry I was late," I said to Jan as we walked toward the north side of the park.

Jan grinned. "I bet the store owners are lined up on the sidewalk, waiting for us. We'd better hurry and get there before they send out a search party."

I laughed and started to feel better. This was more like the typical Saturday afternoon I'd expected. We reached the edge of the park, then crossed Commerce Street. We just made it to the mall side before the light changed.

To the right, I noticed Katrina Betz heading toward us, dressed in the same style long skirt and blue blouse that she always wore. I wondered whether she had a whole closet filled with identical outfits.

Jan and I said hi. I didn't really know Katrina, but I'm not one of those snobs who won't say hi to people who aren't popular. Katrina glanced up, then rushed past us. Instead of going into the mall, she turned toward the crosswalk and stepped off the curb without even looking at the light.

"Watch out!" I shouted.

To our left, a bus hurtled down the road, heading straight toward a meeting with Katrina.

Three

AFTERMATH

When they give us those word problems in math class, I never have a clue what's going on. You know—a bus is racing along at thirty-seven miles an hour toward a badly dressed girl who's crossing the street at four miles an hour. Then they ask how much the driver weighs or what's the length of the bus.

This wasn't math class. This was real life. My brain must have figured out that I could reach Katrina in time. I checked for cars, then raced into the street.

I caught up with Katrina and grabbed her shoulder. She slipped from my grip as I yanked back. But I guess I slowed her down enough. A blast of air and a hot puff of smelly diesel exhaust hit my face as the bus whipped past. We were so close, I don't think the driver even saw us.

"Are you trying to get killed?" I shouted at Katrina

as I brushed the windblown hair out of my eyes. Then I clamped my mouth shut. I realized I sounded just like a parent.

Before I could say anything else, Katrina scurried away toward the park.

"Wow," Jan said when I got back to the sidewalk. "You saved her life. You're a hero."

I shook my head. The rest of my body shook on its own. "She'd have seen the bus. I didn't do anything special. Come on, let's get inside."

We went to the main entrance. "Check it out," Jan said, pointing at an announcement over the doors.

I read the sign out loud: "MALLWIDE MIDNIGHT MAD-NESS SALE THIS TUESDAY—ELEVEN P.M. TO ONE A.M." Perfect. There was no school Wednesday, Thursday, or Friday because of a teachers' conference, so I figured Mom would let me stay up late Tuesday.

Jan walked over to the community bulletin board and found a spot for her poster. "Which way should we go?" she asked as she looked around.

Lewington Mall is built sort of like a wagon wheel with five spokes. Someone with no imagination named the spokes North Mall, South Mall, and so on. That could have been a problem, with five corridors and only four directions, but they called the fifth one Main Mall, even though it's shorter than the others. From above, I'd guess the whole place looks like a turtle.

The front door leads right to the Hub—that's the center area—where there's a fountain and a stream.

People throw pennies in the fountain and make wishes. Some slobs also throw gum wrappers and sales slips into the water. I could make a wish about what should happen to those people.

Except for some litter, the hub is very nice. The mall owners are always adding new decorations. At the moment, a bunch of workers were carrying in plants and setting them up next to the fountain. Another guy was adjusting the fountain so part of the spray would hit the leaves of the plants. Even though it's indoors, the Hub is a great place for trees and flowers. The ceiling over the Hub is a big glass dome that lets in lots of light.

There's a wooden bridge over the stream. It's a perfect spot to check out everything. You can see who's in all the corridors. I headed toward the top of the bridge, but I didn't make it. Something was very wrong. I leaned against the railing and grabbed the polished wood with both hands. Oh, no . . .

"What's the matter?" Jan asked.

"I don't know." My stomach was twisting around like someone was using it to practice tying knots. I stumbled toward Jan. Wow. The moment I got off the bridge, I felt better.

"You sure you're okay?" Jan asked.

"I'm fine. Honest." And I was. Just like that, the bad feeling went away. "Where do you want to go?"

"How about East Mall?" Jan asked. "We could look at swimsuits in Sharon's Sports Shack. I guess all I can do is look. I only brought six dollars."

"Sounds good." Our gym class was going to use the high school pool on Monday. Mom said my old suit was perfectly fine, but at least I could look at new ones.

I glanced toward the entrance to East Mall. It was empty except for one person—May Mellon. She was easy to spot in a bright yellow shirt decorated with purple and green parrots, and a pair of orange pants. But it wasn't her taste in clothes that worried me. There's this poem that called April "the cruelest month." It's by the same man who wrote all those poems about cats. I don't know what it's supposed to mean or why he picked on April—I just saw it in one of Mom's books   but the person who wrote those words had never met May.

"Let's save East Mall for later," I told Jan.

"Oh, yeah," Jan said. "It's the meanest of the Mellons. Hard to believe there are more at home like her."

I nodded. Amazingly enough, May was one of a set of triplets. Her brothers Clem and Clyde were also in our class. They weren't as nasty, but they were pretty rude and crude. She also had tons of other brothers and sisters, including two who went to school with my brother Sebastian. I turned away from May. I had better things to do than to dwell on Mellons. "Where now?" I asked Jan.

She looked toward West Mall. "I've got it!"

I knew what she had in mind. There weren't any good clothing stores in West Mall, but there was one place we both loved. I grinned back at Jan and we said the name together: "Kitty, Kitty, Coo."

Okay—it was a stupid name, but it kind of made sense for a pet store. They had a picture of two kittens and a dove on the sign painted on the window. In real life, I don't think a dove would hang around with kittens, but you're allowed to make stuff up for ads. Jan and I loved looking at the kittens and puppies. If the nice owner was there, we got to hold the kittens and pet the puppies. If the nasty owner was there, we couldn't hold the pets, but we could still look at them until he chased us out and yelled at us for not buying anything. That wasn't fair. Since I didn't have any pets, I can't see how he expected me to buy stuff.

We hurried down West Mall, past Miller's Fat-Free Donuts (icky), Pretzels with a Twist (crunchy), Wrench City (boring), the empty place where the video store had gone out of business ages ago, two nail salons, three hair salons, the empty place where the popcorn store had gone out of business two years ago, and the ninety-eight-cent store that had taken over the ninety-nine-cent store in the spot where the dollar store used to be.

"We're in luck," Jan said when we reached the front of Kitty, Kitty, Coo.

"We sure are," I said when I saw that the nice owner was there. "It's our lucky day."

In less than a minute, I learned how wrong those words could be.

Four

TROUBLE IN STORE

"Oh, look, they are soooo adorable," Jan said, rushing over to the cages stacked along one wall.

Every kitten in the place gazed at us; every pair of eyes begged, *Take us home. We are really, really cute.*

I hurried to the kittens. Across the shop, a scurrying bundle of puppies in their own cages stared at us in disbelief. I guess they couldn't understand how we could possibly visit the kittens first.

Birds in cages over our heads flapped and fluttered, but I think they knew they were stuck in third place. Birds are nice, but you can't really play with them or take them for a walk. Well, I guess you could take them for a flight, but I bet it would be a bad idea.

I went up to the first cage of kittens, unable to keep the *oo00hhh*s and *aaawwwww*s from spilling out of my mouth. "They are so cute," I said. "It's a shame they have to be locked up."

Jan nodded. "My parents made a poster about that last month. It said: FREE THE PETS. They put it up on a tree in front of the house, and people kept ringing our bell and asking about the free pets."

I put my hand on the corner of the first cage. I swear, that's all I did. I didn't bang it or thump it or anything. When I touched the metal, I got a shock, like I'd scuffed my feet on a carpet. I jerked my hand back right away.

I have no idea how the cage door fell open.

It just flipped right down. So did every other door on every other kitten cage. One after the other—*clickita-clackita*—they dropped like toppling dominoes.

I stood there with my mouth open.

The kittens were a lot smarter. They didn't stand around.

It wouldn't have been so bad if it was just the kittens. They scampered through the store, but they didn't try to hide or escape. At least, they didn't until a couple of seconds later, when the puppies got out.

That wasn't my fault, either. I barely bumped the puppy cages. There wasn't any spark this time. But the water in one of the dog bowls splashed up and hit the cage door. There was no way the water could have knocked open the door. But it did. Then all the other dog doors swung down.

And I hardly even touched the birdcages. But when

26

I brushed against them, the birds got startled and fluttered their wings. Somehow, that blew open the doors.

Everyone in the store helped out. The dogs and cats were a lot easier to catch than the birds. But we finally got them all.

"Well, that was fun," Jan said as she put the last parakeet back in its cage. "Maybe we can do it again next week."

"Ouch!" Something sharp was digging into my calf through my jeans. "Well, hi, there," I said, looking down at the cutest little face. A solid black kitten with green eyes had fastened itself to my pants. I tried to pull it free, but it wouldn't let go of my leg. And once I'd touched it, I didn't want to let go, either. It felt so wonderfully soft and alive.

"Seems like someone wants to go home with you," the owner said.

I shook my head. "I don't think my parents would let me."

"You never know until you ask," Jan said.

"You're right." As I spoke those words, the kitten released my leg. I noticed the sign next to the cages. Kittens were only ten dollars. Like many of the puppies, the kittens had been rescued from shelters, so the store didn't charge a lot for them. Still, it was amazing—who'd have thought you could buy total happiness for so little money?

"You have excellent taste," the owner said. "She's the

prettiest kitten in the store. I had a feeling she'd end up with someone special."

"She?" I asked. Now I knew I had to take her. We girls needed to stick together.

"Wrap her up," Jan said.

"Jan!"

"Just kidding. This is great. I'll even treat for some food or something." She pulled a five-dollar bill from her pocket. Then she looked at the owner and asked, "Do you sell mice?"

"Jan!" I said again before I realized she wasn't serious.

Even with Jan chipping in for the food, I still ended up spending a lot more than ten dollars. I bought a small litter box, two bowls, a collar, and three cat toys. It all just fit in my backpack.

"Hang on," Jan said as we left the store. She stopped at a gumball machine. A sign on the front of it said: YOUR DONATION HELPS AID PEOPLE IN NEED. There were machines like that all over the mall. I watched as Jan pulled four quarters from her pocket and started putting them in the coin slot. With each twist of the knob, she got two or three pieces of gum.

"Hey, isn't that your last dollar?" I asked.

Jan shrugged. "It's a good cause." She looked down at the gumballs in her hand. "Want some?"

"Nope. They look like those hot cinnamon ones."

"Yuck. You're right." She turned toward a little kid who was running by. "Here," she said, handing him a double fistful of gumballs. "All yours. Go wild."

"Thanks, lady," the kid said. He took the gum and dashed off. I guess to a little kid, seventh-graders like Jan and me were old enough to be ladies.

"I like sharing," Jan said with a grin. "Especially when I'm sharing something I don't like." Then she pointed at my new pet. "So, what are you going to call her?"

"I don't know." I held up my kitten and looked in her eyes, trying to decide what her name should be. The owner had wanted to put her in a cardboard pet carrier, but I needed to hold her in my arms. "Something special. I'll know the right name when I think of it."

We walked back through West Mall toward the Hub.

"Uh-oh," Jan said, looking toward the donut shop. "There's May."

"She's busy window-shopping," I said. I figured we could sneak past without attracting her attention. She probably liked teasing kittens as much as she liked picking on kids.

Then I saw that May had spotted someone else, and I knew there was going to be trouble.

Five

BULLY FOR HER

As I looked into the Hub beyond West Mall, I saw Katrina plop down on a bench. I guess she'd come back from the park. May turned away from the donuts and headed toward her target.

"She's doomed," Jan said. "This is like those nature films, where the bunny is sitting on the grass, all peaceful and happy. You know, then the camera pulls back and there's a hawk or a fox getting ready for dinner. The poor kid is about to get pounced on."

"We have to do something," I said. "You distract May, and I'll get Katrina out of there."

"Me?" Jan asked. "No way. You distract her."

"I thought of it first," I said.

Jan shook her head.

There wasn't any time to argue. I rushed past May and ran to Katrina.

"Hi!" I said, grabbing her hand.

She looked up at me, startled.

"Come on," I said, tugging at her. "Time to go." I got her on her feet. It wasn't easy with a kitten in one hand and a loaded pack on my back.

Jan ran over to join us. She grabbed Katrina's other hand. "Hurry."

We dragged her along as fast as we could. Then I looked over my shoulder.

May was still following us. It reminded me of those scary movies where the victim keeps running away, while the monster slowly chases her. Somehow, the monster always catches up.

As I looked for the best way out, I saw three things that had nothing to do with each other—yet somehow they connected in my mind. The little kid with the gumballs was running wild through the Hub. Near May, a mall worker was struggling to carry a large pot of flowers. Between us and May, a worker at the edge of the fountain was tightening a water pipe with a wrench.

"That kid can't keep running forever," I said.

"What?" Jan asked.

"Nothing."

Just then, the kid stopped running. He stood there, panting. But he made the mistake of standing right in front of May. She reached out and pushed him away. He shouted and threw a handful of gumballs at her. They just bounced off May like pebbles off a battleship and scattered across the floor. The guy carrying the pot slipped on one. The pot went flying. It landed with a crash in front of May, spilling dirt in a pile.

The man with the wrench must have been startled by the crash. He jerked too hard and broke the valve. Water shot from the pipe, spraying right into the pile of dirt. It turned into instant mud that splashed up and covered May with a sheet of brown goo.

"Let's go," I said, dragging Katrina to the edge of the Hub and down Main Mall. I kept going until we were out of sight of May, but I didn't think she was following us anymore. She had other things on her mind. And on her face, and on her clothes . . .

"Hey," I said to Katrina. "Don't you know when there's danger heading toward you?"

"That girl is *not* nice," Jan said.

For the first time, Katrina spoke. "The girl back there? I don't think she'd do anything to me. Did you see her shirt? You know, she always wears the prettiest clothes."

"Yeah, right," I said. "Look, we have to get going. Just be careful, okay?"

Katrina looked down at the ground, then back at me. "Beautiful kitten," she said. "Isn't she a darling?"

"Yeah, she is," I said. As Katrina walked away, her words caught in my mind. "Darling . . ." I studied my kitten. "What do you think?" I asked her, lifting her up so we could see into each other's eyes. "Are you Darling?"

"Mewwww," Darling said, telling me she liked her name.

33

"I guess I'd better go home. Want to come over?" I asked Jan.

She shook her head. "No thanks. I don't want to be around when you explain this. Your folks will probably blame me. The way they act, you'd think I was always giving you bad ideas."

"Well, what about the time we used my mom's roasting pan to tie-dye T-shirts? Remember? That was your idea."

Jan shrugged. "I still don't see the problem. So what if the next roast chicken came out with purple gravy? Purple is such a pretty color."

"And how about the time you said we could make a great drink with orange juice and baking soda?" I asked.

"That was *years* ago," Jan said. "Besides, it should have worked."

I shuddered as I remembered the way it had foamed up and splattered all over the counter. "I'm still finding sticky spots in the kitchen."

"Okay, maybe I've given you one or two bad ideas. But you can't say that about your little Darling."

"Nope. You're right—she's definitely a great idea."

Jan walked with me down to the end of Main Mall. "Mellon alert," she said when we reached the exit.

I watched as Clem and Clyde tried to come inside. They were fighting over who was going to go through the door first. Every time one of them started to step in, the other would grab him and yank him back.

People were staring at them and walking around to the other doors.

"At least they never bother us," I said to Jan. I was pretty sure those two had no idea who I was, and I liked it that way.

"Yeah. They're too busy bothering each other," she said.

I said good-bye to Jan, then crossed the street and headed home.

Just my luck, when I reached my house, I ran into Sebastian. His friends call him Splat, for some reason I don't remember. I call him a pest. Sometimes we get along, but he's always picking fights with me.

"Hey," Sebastian said. "Is that a cat?"

"Hey," I said back, "I guess you really did learn something in school. Maybe next week they'll teach you to recognize doggies. Duh."

"I see one right now," he said. "Woof, woof."

"You are such a child."

"And you're in so much trouble." He turned toward the house. "Angie has a cat," he whispered. "Angie has a cat," he said a little more loudly. Then he said it again, even louder.

"Stop that. Don't ruin this for me."

He said it again, almost shouting.

"Stop. I'm warning you."

He smiled and shook his head. Then he took a real deep breath, like he was going to scream at the top of his lungs.

"You wouldn't dare," I said.

"*Angie has—!*"

I grabbed his shoulder. "Stop!"

There was no question about the shock this time. It knocked my hand away from Sebastian. I looked at my fingers, expecting to see some kind of burn marks. But everything was fine. I looked back at Sebastian.

He wasn't there. My brother had vanished.

Six

THE PERFECT BROTHER

"Sebastian?" I called. "Come on. Stop hiding." He couldn't have run off that quickly. But he must have. There was no other explanation. At least he wasn't going to spoil my chance to tell Mom about Darling. I started to walk toward the porch.

"Yeeeoowwrrlll!" Darling let out a screech and dug her kitten claws into my shoulder.

"Hey! That hurt." That's when I glanced down. I'd almost stepped on a doll. *A doll?* I knelt and stared at the doll that was lying on the ground. It had a rag body and a porcelain head. And it looked like Sebastian. It looked *exactly* like him—same clothes and everything.

"It can't be . . . ," I whispered.

"Mewwwp," Darling said.

I touched the doll with one finger. I almost expected

37

it to be warm and breathing, but it felt like any other doll. "Sebastian, is that you?" I asked.

It didn't answer. I don't know what I would have done if it had talked. I couldn't leave it outside. I picked up the doll and headed toward the front door.

"Hey, is Splat home?" a voice called from behind me.

"No!" I spun around, thrusting the doll behind my back. "He's not here."

It was Sebastian's friend Norman. The kid was smart. Actually, he was more than just smart. He was stuffed so full of knowledge, I figured he'd explode someday and fill the air with flying numbers and millions of facts. Maybe everyone in the neighborhood would grow a little bit smarter if that happened.

"That's weird," Norman said. "You were obviously entering your house, not leaving it. How could you know Splat isn't there?"

"Sisters just know this sort of thing. He's not inside."

Norman shrugged. "Nice cat. American shorthair variety, I'd say. Probably female. Well, if you see Splat, tell him I came by. He's supposed to come over. We're going to go online and chat with people in Hong Kong tonight. It will be very cool."

"I'm sure it will be fascinating." I turned back toward the house and sneaked inside, making sure Mom wasn't in sight. I rushed up to my room and put the doll on my dresser.

"This is crazy," I told Darling. "That can't be my brother. There's an explanation. Right?"

39

Darling didn't give me an answer. I put her on the bed. She padded over to my pillow and plopped down. "Welcome to your new home," I said as I took her bowls and litter box out of my backpack. "At least, I hope it will be your home. We'll find out in a minute." I wanted to tell Mom about Darling right away. Then I could try to figure out what to do about the doll.

I picked Darling up and went downstairs.

"Mom?" I called.

"I'm in here," she called back.

I followed her voice to the living room. She was dusting the stereo speakers. Her back was to me. I took a deep breath. "Need any help?" I asked.

"Thanks, but I'm almost finished."

"Can I get you a glass of juice?" I asked.

She shook her head. "No thanks."

"Want me to make dinner tonight?"

"It's already made."

"I could polish the silverware."

"I polished it yesterday."

"Like my new kitten?" I asked. "Her name's Darling."

"She's adorable," Mom said as she glanced over her shoulder. She turned back toward the speakers. Before I could even start my escape, she whirled around. "Kitten! What's going on here?"

The words spilled out. "Oh, Mom, she's just so cute and she wouldn't let go of me and when I looked in her eyes, I knew I had to bring her home and didn't you ever feel that way like when I was a baby or something and she's so sweet so *pleeeaaase* can I keep her if I promise to do all the work?"

Mom sneezed.

I had a terrible thought. "You aren't allergic, are you?"

She pointed to the speakers and said, "Just to dust."

"So can I keep her?" If she said no, I knew I was doomed. But maybe she'd say the other thing.

Mom spoke. "We'll have to see what your father says."

Yes! I knew what that meant. This was Mom's way of giving me permission without actually admitting she was giving me permission. Even better, Dad was away until Wednesday. That meant Darling had plenty of time for Mom to get attached to her. By Thursday, we'd be one big, happy, cat-loving family.

"Thanks, Mom. I mean it. Really. This will be great."

She held up a hand. "Don't get too excited. We have to ask your father."

"Sure. Yeah. I realize that." But I knew exactly what Dad would do. He'd sigh and look at Mom, and then say, *Well, if it's okay with your mother, I guess it's okay with me.*

"By the way," Mom said as I left the room, "have you seen Sebastian?"

"Isn't he going to Norman's?"

Mom nodded. "I hadn't realized he'd already left."

"I'll keep an eye out for him." I headed toward the stairs.

As I reached the first step, my little brother Rory

41

called out from the top of the landing, "Angie, where'd you get this?"

I looked up and gasped. Rory was dangling the doll over the banister.

Seven

SOME THINGS NEVER CHANGE

I put Darling down. "Don't drop it!"

"Where'd you get this?" Rory asked again. "It looks like Sebastian." He swung the doll back and forth by one leg, then tossed it into the air and said, "Wheeeee." He caught it by an arm.

I raced up the steps. Rory tossed the doll again, higher than before. It bounced out of his hand when he tried to catch it. I leaned over the railing and made a grab. I just managed to get my fingers around one foot.

I glared at Rory. "Who said you could go into my room?"

"Sorry." He started to get that rubbery look on his face like he was going to cry.

"Hey, that's okay. I'm not angry," I said. "Just ask first. Look, want to see my kitten?"

"Kitten?"

"Her name's Darling." I pointed to her as she climbed up the steps. She padded over to Rory and batted at his perpetually dangling shoelaces. He giggled. I went to my room and put Sebastian back on the dresser, then returned to the hall. Darling and Rory were getting to know each other.

Rory looked up at me. "Did Mom say you could keep her?"

"Mom said she'd have to ask Dad."

Rory grinned. "That means you can keep her."

"I know." I grinned, too. But then my grin faded. I felt great about Darling, but I was worried about the strange stuff that was going on. I'd turned Sebastian into a doll. Normally, that would be a useful talent, but I really wished I knew how to turn him back. He could be a huge pain, but he was my brother. And I guess we'd gotten closer after that vampire thing that had happened to him a few months ago.

Maybe that was it!

Maybe I hadn't caused the change. It could be some side effect from what he'd been through.

The doorbell rang. "Rory," Mom called a moment later, "Becky is here."

"Got to go," Rory said. "We're building a rocket ship so we can fly to Mars. Thanks for letting me play with your kitten." He ran down the steps to join his friend.

"Life's so easy when you're little," I told Darling as I scooped her into my arms. "That kid doesn't have a problem in the world. Just eat, sleep, and play. Kind of like you." I held her next to my cheek and felt the gentle rumble of her purring. "Now, I, on the other hand, have problems."

I went back in my room and closed the door. "Okay," I said, looking at the doll, "change back." I touched it on the shoulder with my right hand. Nothing happened. I touched the other shoulder. I tried using my left hand.

"Abracadabra," I said, feeling more than a little foolish. "Hocus-pocus. Ala kazam." No luck. The doll was still a doll.

"I command you to change."

Nope.

"I command *thee* to change."

No luck.

The phone rang.

"Could you get that?" Mom called from downstairs.

I picked it up in my parents' room.

"Is Splat there?" Norman asked.

"He can't come tonight," I said.

"Why?"

What could I say? *I turned him into a doll and I'm having a little trouble turning him back. I can bring him over, but he won't be great company. All he's good for is a tea party.* Nope. I don't think so.

"Never mind," Norman said before I could think of a reasonable excuse. "I guess something better came along. I understand." He hung up the phone.

Now I felt even worse. Norman probably figured

Sebastian had ditched him for the evening. Before I'd met Jan, I had some friends who weren't always very nice to me. I knew what it felt like to get dumped. My hand hovered over the phone, but I couldn't do it. I especially couldn't tell Norman that there was a problem I couldn't solve. Not until I'd tried my hardest to figure it out by myself.

I went back to my room, sat on my bed, and lifted Darling up to my face. "What is going on?" I asked her. "Do you have any idea what's happening to me?"

"Mewrowp."

That was all the answer I got from her.

I tried everything I could think of to change Sebastian back. Nothing worked. That evening, after dinner, I tried some more. Eventually, I started getting suspicious. Maybe Sebastian was playing some kind of a joke on me. It wouldn't surprise me if he and Norman had rigged the whole thing up somehow. There was no way the doll could really be my brother.

It didn't matter. By then, I was so tired, I knew I had to stop trying and get ready for bed.

That's when the bad part started.

Eight

OUT OF CONTROL

As I reached for my hairbrush, it shot from my hand and smashed into the wall. The brush shattered into tiny pieces. It was so sudden and unexpected, I just froze for a moment.

Instead of falling, the pieces rose up, buzzing like insects, and flew around the room in a swarm. They kept circling my head. As I tried to get away from them, I noticed movement on my bed. The pillow was jerking and shaking, like there was something alive inside the case. With each jerk, it moved closer to the edge of the bed.

"Stop." I wanted to shout, but the word came out in a whisper.

The pillow reached the edge of the bed and started to topple to the floor.

I backed away until I felt the dresser pressing against

me. The pillow fell from the bed. It hit the floor and splashed open, spilling a thick green liquid on the rug. The pieces of the brush flew away from me and swooped onto the puddle.

The drawer behind me shot open, pushing me across the room. I barely managed to stop before stepping into the spreading green puddle.

I spun toward the dresser just as Darling leaped up there.

I took a step toward her. One of my shirts moved inside the open drawer. The sleeve lifted up and flapped over the edge. Something swelled inside it and started to come out. Fingers. A hand. It slithered through the sleeve. The index finger pointed at me.

"No. Stop. Please . . . stop."

Around the room, orange light flickered, throwing fireplace shadows on the walls. I felt heat and smelled smoke.

My curtains lifted as a breeze entered the room, even though the window was closed. The breeze gained force. I closed my eyes. The wind blew hard particles against my face. It felt like sand. An instant later, I flinched as a crash of thunder shook the house. The air grew damp as the wind drove rain into the room.

Inside my head, I heard a voice. *Earth, air, fire, and water. Choose your power, chosen daughter.*

I looked at the doll, expecting it to leap up or start talking. It didn't move.

All the clothing in the open dresser drawer flew into the air as lightning struck again.

A third bolt hit so close to the house that I could feel my hair standing out from my head as the air filled with static electricity.

The light grew brighter. Lightning hit twice more, coming so quickly that the second thunderclap overlapped the first. Then the whole world—the light and sound and the wind against my face—faded, growing dimmer and weaker, moving farther away. The world turned gray, then darker. The sounds became whispers. The whispers became silence. I crumpled to the floor and slipped into the blackness.

Nine

IN A REAL MESS

Someone was rubbing my face with a rough washcloth.

No. It was Darling, licking my face.

I sat up slowly, expecting more terror, but the room was quiet. I found my brush on the floor. It wasn't shattered, but there was a crack in the handle. My pillow was undamaged, but it smelled of mildew. My clothes were scattered around the room.

I piled the clothes in the corner. I wasn't sure I wanted to put anything in that drawer. What a terrible night! I headed down to the kitchen. As I passed the stove, the left front burner burst into flames. I turned the knob, shutting off the gas.

Earth, air, fire, and water. The voice rose in my mind.

"No," I said aloud. "Not again. Stop this."

There was a rush of water from the faucet behind me. I turned it off. The gas flared up again. Then the faucet. The fan above the oven started spinning. I heard a rattle. The windows shook. Glass came from sand. Sand was from the earth.

Earth, air, fire, and water. Choose your power, chosen daughter. It was a chorus of voices now.

If I had to choose, what would I pick? Fire can burn you. Earth can bury you. Water can drown you. "Air," I said, though I had no idea what it meant. The moment I spoke, the flame died, the water stopped, and the rattling ended. The fan kept running. I reached out and switched it off.

Darling stretched her front paws up my leg. "I have to go out," I told her. "I need to find some answers."

"Meewworlll."

I guess that meant it was okay.

I headed for Jan's house. For all her silliness and joking around, Jan comes up with some great ideas. She's got a lot more common sense than most people realize.

In a way, we make a strange pair. It's like we're riding bikes to the same spot on a mountain, but Jan is coasting downhill while I'm pedaling up the slope. I'll work for days on a report. Jan will write something at the last minute. We'll both get a B. I'll spend a half hour choosing an outfit to wear. Jan will grab some clothes from her floor, and she'll look great. But that doesn't bother me. She's my friend.

I reached her house and rang the bell.

Jan came to the door, gasped, and said, "You look absolutely awful."

I could also count on her to be disgustingly honest. "I had a rough night."

"What's going on?" Jan asked when we got to her room.

"Something real spooky is happening to me," I said.

"Great. I love spooky stuff."

"This isn't fun spooky." I told her about the park.

Jan frowned. "After you saw the lady become a bird, did you see anything else? Dancing fairies? Juggling trolls? Elvis Presley in a flying saucer?"

"I'm serious," I told her. "I think I can do things."

"That's great," Jan said. "Do something."

"I don't know how." I looked around, wishing that something would happen. Across the room, behind Jan, half the clothes in her closet slithered off their hangers and dropped to the floor. "Look!" I said.

Jan glanced over and shrugged. "So I'm a bit messy. That's not exactly news."

"I'm not making this up."

"I believe you," Jan said. "You don't have to show me any proof."

"Really?" It felt great to hear those words.

Jan nodded. "Sure. I mean, you'd believe anything I told you. Right?"

"Right." I guess that's part of why we were friends.

Jan smiled and said, "You know, it would be so cool to have some kind of special power. Think about it, Angie."

I shook my head. "It's not cool. I don't have any control. I don't know what's going to happen next."

"But imagine what you could do if you learned to control the power. You could save the rain forests. You could feed all the hungry people in the world."

"No," I said, shaking my head again. "Don't you think if someone could do that sort of stuff, it would be done already?"

"Maybe the wrong person had the power? . . ."

Wow. I didn't know what to say to that. I certainly felt like the wrong person.

"Hey," Jan said, "if you can't save the planet, what about creating a couple of triple scoop hot fudge sundaes. Extra fudge. Nuts. Two cherries. No calories. That can't be too hard."

"This isn't like some old TV show. I can't just blink stuff up like a genie. Right now, all I want is to figure out what's going on, and get my life back in control."

Jan nodded. "Okay. We'll save the sundaes for later. First some control. Then the rain forest. And then the sundaes. Where should we start?"

"I was hoping you'd have an idea."

She snapped her fingers. "We could call the power company."

"That's not very helpful," I said.

"What about a fortune-teller?" Jan asked. "You know, like in that house over on Randi Street with the sign in the window."

"I don't think those people are for real." I knew the place she meant. The sign showed a picture of a hand and a crystal ball. I had a feeling the owner was the only

one who ended up with any kind of fortune. But that gave me an idea. "Isn't there a shop that sells magic stuff over on Castor Avenue?"

Jan nodded. "Yeah, right down the block from the yarn store. It's got a funny name. I know— it's the Good Speller."

"Let's go." I hopped off Jan's bed. As we left her room, I glanced back. The sheet rose from her mattress as if being puffed up from beneath by air. "Jan! Your bed!" I pointed toward it, but by the time she looked, it had fallen back down.

"Hey," she said, "you're starting to act like my mom. If you want my help, stop bugging me about the mess in my room. Deal?"

"Deal."

We hurried down to Castor Street. The Good Speller was at the end of the block. Beneath the name, the sign said: SPELLS, POTIONS, AMULETS, AND BOOKS. According to another sign, they also sold lottery tickets and repaired window shades. At the very bottom was the owner's name—MISS ZENOBIA CHUTNEY.

A bell tinkled as I opened the door. The place was pretty dark. "Hello?" I called.

A plump woman with gray hair and glasses stood up from behind a counter on the left side of the store. "Lucinda!" she called, rushing around the counter. "It's you!"

She ran toward me. Then she stopped, took a good look at me, and fainted.

Ten

EXPERT HELP?

I tried to catch the lady as she dropped to the floor. I didn't quite break her fall, but I slowed it down a little.

"What should we do?" I asked Jan.

"Raise her feet?"

"You sure?" That didn't seem right to me.

Jan frowned. "Raise her head?"

"Stop guessing."

"I know—let's raise her feet and her head."

"Jan!"

I looked down at the woman. She opened one eye, peeked up at me, then closed it again.

"Lady," I said, "what's going on?"

She scrunched her eyes tighter.

"Come on. I really need some help. Please."

She opened one eye again. Then she opened the other. She looked like she wanted to run away from me.

"Could I have some water?" she asked Jan. "There's a sink in the back."

"Sure." Jan got up and went through a door behind the counter.

"Relax," I told the woman. "I won't hurt you. Honest."

She shook her head. "This is a very dangerous time. Whether you want to or not, you might hurt yourself or those around you."

"No. I'd never hurt anyone."

"Yes, you might."

There was a clink from the next room, followed by the sound of water running. I realized that this woman had sent Jan off so she could talk to me alone. "Who is Lucinda? My name's Angelina Claypool. Why'd you think I was Lucinda?"

"That's not important right now. But I must know one thing: Are you a good person?"

"Of course I am." I blurted that out without even thinking. How else could I answer that question?

"Here we go," Jan said as she came back. "Here's a nice cold glass of water for you." She glanced at me. "Cold is good, right? We don't want hot water. That's for delivering a baby."

The woman sat up and took the glass. "Thank you, dearie."

"Are you Miss Chutney?" I asked.

"Yes. That's me." She put down the glass and rubbed her hands together.

"Can you tell me anything about power?"

She still looked scared. But she also looked like she wanted to talk. "I don't mean to boast," she said, "but I am considered quite an expert when it comes to—"

The bell rang as the door opened. The most beautiful woman I'd ever seen walked into the shop. If someone took all the best in me and all the best in Jan and all the best in every other girl in our class and put it together, the result wouldn't have been half as pretty as this woman. I heard Jan give a little gasp. I heard myself give a little gasp, too.

"I'd like some service, please," the woman said. She looked at Miss Chutney, apparently unsurprised to find the store owner sitting on the floor. Then she looked at me. I felt like I'd been placed under a microscope.

"Girls," Miss Chutney said, "run along now." She rose from the floor and stood between me and the beautiful woman. Her voice had dropped to almost a whisper. "This is no place for you young ladies."

"But . . ." I couldn't believe she was throwing us out.

"Please leave," she said, making a shooing motion at us like we were flies. "I have a business to run."

"Come on, Claypool," Jan said, taking my arm and trying to sound like a cowboy. "We aren't welcome in these here parts." She started to drag me from the shop.

I didn't want to leave—I wanted answers. But Jan was tugging at me, and Miss Chutney had turned her attention to the new customer. There didn't seem to be any point in trying to stay.

"Now what?" Jan asked as the door closed behind us and we walked away from the shop.

I had no idea. "Maybe I'll just go home."

"Or we could go to the mall," Jan said.

Before I could answer, I heard a shout from behind us. "Wait!"

I turned back. Miss Chutney came huffing out of the store, waving a bag. "You forgot your book." She ran up and thrust the package toward me.

I just stared at her.

"Take it," Miss Chutney said.

"Uh, thanks." I took the bag from her.

She turned back toward her shop and left us standing on the sidewalk.

I opened the bag and slid the book out. It was a small, thin volume, covered with cracked leather that smelled like the furniture in our attic.

"Let's see," Jan said.

I held up the book so she—and I—could read the cover. The title was *The Passage of Power*.

"Not exactly a light romance," Jan said.

She was right about that. But maybe it had some answers. There was still a problem, though. I was leaving the store with something besides the book. I was leaving with another question—one I'd never even wondered about before today. "Jan?" I asked.

"What?"

"Do you think I'm a good person?"

Eleven

ANSWERS AND QUESTIONS

I guess I expected Jan to say *Of course you're good*. Instead, she said, "Do *you* think you're a good person?"

"I asked you first."

"It depends what you mean by *good*," she said.

"That's not a very helpful answer," I told her.

"It's not a very easy question," she said.

She was right. It was a tough question. I wasn't even sure what it meant to be good. I mean, I mostly listened to my folks, and I didn't get into trouble in school. But I don't think that's what Miss Chutney had in mind.

"So," Jan said, "let's get back to my question: Want to go to the mall?"

I clutched the book. I needed to read it, but I knew Jan wanted to go to the mall. Well, there were nice places to sit in the mall and read. It would be real rotten of me to dump her and go home after she'd been so nice about coming to the Good Speller with me.

"Yeah," I said. "The mall would be great."

Jan grinned at me. "There's your answer."

"What do you mean?"

"This proves you're a good person."

We walked through town toward the mall. On Taylor Street, a couple of blocks from the spell shop, a guy was washing his car in his driveway. The water ran in a soapy stream to the street and into the gutter. When I tried to step over the water, I got that same sick feeling I'd gotten on the bridge in the mall.

Jan looked back at me and asked, "Afraid to get your shoes wet?"

"Just being careful," I told her as I walked into the street and went around the water.

"Home at last," Jan said when we reached the mall. "Where do you want to go first?"

"How about we sit in the Hub for a while? I'd like to look at my book."

Jan made a face. "Gosh, that sounds like tons of fun. I can watch you read. If I'm good, will you let me turn the pages?"

"Okay. You choose," I said, feeling guilty.

"Greeting cards?" Jan asked. "My grandma's birthday is next week."

"Sure."

We headed to the card shop. While Jan looked through the choices, I sneaked a peek at my book. The first part explained how power itself wasn't good or bad. What mattered was the way people used power. I guess that made sense. I mean, you could use gasoline to drive someone to the library or to start a fire. You could do good things with electricity, like light a room, or bad things, like give someone a shock.

The one sentence in the book that really got me thinking was: *Power seeks its rightful owner.* The woman in the park must have gone there to pass on her power, but I doubt it was meant for me. Maybe the rightful owner would try to find me.

"Move!"

I'd been standing in an aisle, reading. Someone pushed me aside and walked past. "Hey, don't be so pushy," I said before I realized who I was talking to.

"What did you say?" May asked, turning slowly back toward me like an oil tanker moving out of a harbor.

"Nothing." I thought how nice it would be to blast her with some of my power. I imagined changing her into a pig. I could just see her running around on four legs, still wearing that tacky outfit. The thought made me smile.

"You laughing at me?" she asked, balling the fingers of her right hand into a fist the size of a canned ham.

I shook my head.

"Take it back," May ordered. "I'm *not* pushy." As she said this, she reached out and pushed my shoulder.

"I take it back," I said as my amusement was replaced by fear. "You're not pushy."

"That's better." She glared at me, and I think she still wanted to hit me just for the fun of it.

But then the breeze drifted in. And on the breeze was the most marvelous aroma. Pies. Fresh-baked pies. May looked. I looked. Outside, just past the entrance to the card shop, a man pushed a cart displaying a sign that said: MRS. NYE'S HOUSE OF PIES. FREE SAMPLES.

May didn't even glance back at me. She dashed off. The moment she left, the breeze stopped.

I noticed Jan standing off to the side. "That was close," she said.

I nodded.

"I never understood how you can take something back," Jan said. "I mean, once it's said, it's said. Right? It's not like you can suck back the words or something. Or maybe you can." She grinned and said, "Pushy." Then she said it backwards. "Eeshup."

"Jan, you're getting weird."

She giggled and kept on saying it. "Pushy, eeshup. Pushy, eeshup. I said it. I took it back. I said it. I took it back."

I was about to tell her how annoying it was when the idea hit me. "That's it," I said, grabbing her arm. "I have to go." I'd realized how to turn the doll back into my brother. Holding tightly to the book, I ran home.

Twelve

DUH

"Mewwp." Darling greeted me in the hallway.

"Hi," I said, scooping her up. "I missed you."

"Merroop."

I guess she missed me, too. I cuddled her as I carried her upstairs. "This has to work," I said, walking over to the dresser where the doll waited patiently for me. I tried to sit it up, but it fell back and hit the wood with a loud *clunk*. I winced and picked up the doll. I didn't see any damage. The head was nice and hard, just like Sebastian's.

I thought back to what had happened right before he changed. I'd grabbed him and shouted, "Stop!" If I'd really caused the change, maybe I just had to reverse things. "Here goes," I said to Darling. "Wish me luck."

I was afraid it wouldn't work. I think I was even more afraid it *would* work. Up until this moment, I hadn't caused anything to happen, except by accident. I took a deep breath. Then I held the doll by the shoulder and shouted, *"Pots!"*

"—a kitten!" Sebastian yelled. He'd changed back in midshout. Whatever had happened to him—whatever *I'd* done to him—had been reversed.

"Angie has a kitten!" he shouted again.

Then his eyes shot wide open and he gasped. I guess it took him a second to realize he wasn't outside. I knew I had to come up with an explanation fast, while he was still confused.

"Whoa!" He looked wildly around.

"Will you stop following me," I said. It was a struggle, but I managed to act as if nothing strange had happened. "You've been shouting that for the last ten minutes. It's really annoying. And get out of my room. Okay?"

"But . . ." Sebastian looked around. Then he grabbed the back of his head with both hands. "Owww. Oh, man, my head really hurts. Whoa—there's a bump on it!"

"If you hadn't been so busy trying to annoy me, you might not have slipped when you were chasing me up the steps," I told him. "You really took a hard hit. I'm surprised you even know where you are."

He gave me a puzzled look. Then he glanced at my clock and said, "Oh, man, I'm late. Norman's waiting for me. I was supposed to be at his house an hour ago. He probably thinks I ditched him." He staggered out of the room, still holding his head.

"Put some ice on it," I called after him. As I heard

the front door slam, I realized no time had passed for him. He still thought it was Saturday. I wasn't looking forward to his reaction when he learned he'd lost a day. If he got mad at me, he'd dedicate his entire life to getting revenge.

There was a chance I could still get out of this. I ran to the phone and dialed Norman's number. Maybe I could make an excuse for Sebastian, so Norman wouldn't tell him what day it was.

"Hello," Norman said.

"Hi. It's Angelina." I paused. This wasn't going to work. Even if I kept Norman from talking about what day it was, Sebastian would still find out soon enough. Especially when Mom woke him up for school tomorrow.

"Well, what do you want?" Norman asked.

I said the first thing that popped into my mind. "What do you know about running water?" I guess the walk to the mall was still bothering me.

"What *don't* I know about running water," he replied. "There's hydroelectric power, of course, and—"

"No, I mean what about crossing running water?"

"Well, the most obvious means is a bridge," Norman said. "But it's funny you should mention running water. There's that old superstition about it, of course."

"What superstition?" I asked.

"You know. Witches can't cross running water."

I almost dropped the phone. "Witches?" I asked.

"Sure. I thought everyone knew that. Hey, I have to

go. Bye." He hung up. I hung up. I walked back to my room, trying to swallow the idea that Norman had handed me.

I looked at Darling. "I'm a witch."

"Mewrrrrlll," she said. I think that's the cat version of "Duh." She hopped onto the floor, as if the topic bored her, and curled up in a patch of sunlight.

A witch . . . I was a witch. . . .

The idea was so ridiculous that I cackled. I mean, I laughed, but it sounded way too much like a witch's cackle. "Stop it," I said aloud.

What next? Should I get a big, black, pointy hat? No way I was going to make that kind of fashion blunder. Was I supposed to start boiling disgusting stuff in a huge iron kettle? Yuck. I thought about that Shakespeare thing, the one with the three witches chanting, "Double double, toil and trouble. Fire burn and cauldron bubble." What was it they put in the pot? Eye of newt? I'm not even sure what a newt is. Some kind of crawly thing. Double yuck.

I looked at myself in the mirror. I didn't seem any different. A witch? I shook my head. "I don't want this. I didn't ask for this."

But as I gazed into the mirror, I noticed the smallest hint of a smile on my lips. Power. I had power. Kids never get any real power. At least, this kid had never had any real power. Until now . . .

Thirteen

BOOK LEARNING

I started reading the book. Darling hopped right up on the bed and draped herself across my legs. In a moment, she was napping.

The book said that there were certain ancient powers that were passed from person to person. There was no way to tell what form the power would take, or how it could be controlled or used. Most of the people who had the power couldn't do much with it. A person might have some small talent for finding lost items or growing large vegetables.

Once in a while, someone with power used it to do great good or great evil. I shuddered as I read about that part. The book warned that evil could even be done by someone trying to do good. Power wasn't a simple gift. I'd certainly learned that already.

The last chapter told about the actual passage of

power. I wasn't happy to learn that power could be stolen. The book said:

He who seeks to steal power must dispatch the holder.

I sort of remembered that a *dispatch* was a letter or a message. I was about to reach for my dictionary when my eyes wandered to the next page. According to the book:

There exist two opportunities for the passage of power.

Power may be passed on the fifth day of possession, in a place of power, at a time of power, before five minutes have flown.

Power must be passed after five times five times five years.

It took me a moment to do the math. Five times five times five . . . *125 years!* I thought about the woman in the park. She'd had her power for a century and a quarter.

I needed to learn more about witches. I looked across the room at my bookcase. Other than *The Lion, the Witch and the Wardrobe* and an old copy of *The Wonderful Wizard of Oz*, there was nothing that might help, and I suspected my answers wouldn't be found in Narnia or Oz. Mom and Dad had lots of books, but they were mostly novels. Rory had Dr. Seuss. Sebastian had comic books. The library was closed on Sunday. The last time I'd typed anything into a search engine, I'd gotten mostly information I knew was wrong.

But Norman had a whole house filled with books. I lifted Darling off my legs and put her back on the bed. She shifted, but she didn't wake up. I rushed over to Norman's place.

"It's open," his mom called when I rang the bell.

I walked in and followed the wonderful smells to the kitchen. Mrs. Weed is a caterer. She had a batch of something fabulous bubbling in a pot on the stove.

"Hello, Angelina," she said. A timer went off. She glanced across the room at a second oven. "Could you stir this for me for a moment? I have to get the rolls out."

"Uh, sure," I said, taking the spoon from her.

"It's coq au vin—a French chicken stew. I'm making it for a party at the Uppersnoot Country Club tomorrow." She dashed to the oven and opened the door. The wonderful smell of baked rolls filled the air.

As I stirred the stew, something floated to the surface. It was small and round and black. Another one appeared next to it. I gagged as I realized I'd just learned what eye of newt looked like. In a moment, the whole surface was filled with them. They bobbed around, staring in a hundred directions. A couple of them popped with wet splashes and sank out of sight. A couple more popped. Then they all started bursting.

"Thanks," Mrs. Weed said, reaching for the spoon as the last eye winked out of sight.

I handed the spoon to her, then looked back in the pot. Everything seemed normal. But I wouldn't want to be dining on coq au vin at the country club tomorrow. No thanks.

"Your brother's upstairs with Norman," Mrs. Weed told me.

"I know. But that's not why I came. I have a report due on witches, and I couldn't get to the library."

"Try the middle bookcase in the living room," Mrs. Weed said. "Second or third shelf, I think. Feel free to borrow whatever you want." She dipped a spoon in the pot, then tasted the broth and made a face. "Hmmm, I guess I went a bit heavy on the salt."

"Thanks." I went to the living room. As I looked through the shelves, I heard Norman and Sebastian arguing upstairs.

"I wish you'd quit moping around just because I was an hour late," Sebastian said. "You've been sulking since I got here."

"An hour?" Norman said to him. "You're a day late. A whole day. You missed everything."

"You're crazy. It's Saturday!" Sebastian shouted.

"Sunday!" Norman shouted back. "Irrefutably, positively Sunday. Look. Right here on the computer. See the date?"

"I don't care about the stupid computer. I know what day it is," Sebastian said.

"Wait right here," Norman told him.

I heard footsteps stomping down the stairs. Norman

75

rushed past me and grabbed something from the table. As he ran past again, I noticed he was carrying the comics. The *Sunday* comics.

I pulled out four books on witches and hurried back into the kitchen.

"Find what you need?" Mrs. Weed asked.

"Yes, thanks again."

"Any time." She glanced at her spoon, tasted the stew once more, and frowned. "That's the last time I buy chicken from Krestner's Market."

I rushed home with the books. I'd just reached the porch when I heard the shout.

"Hold it right there!"

Fourteen

DON'T EVER LEAVE ME

"What's wrong?" I asked, turning to face Sebastian.

"It's Sunday," he said. "Last thing I knew, it was Saturday. Next thing I know—*blam!*—it's Sunday." He looked at the books in my arms. "You did something. I know it."

I took a step back. Sebastian took a step forward.

"What's going on?" He reached for the books.

"No!" I yelled, grabbing his arm.

Shock.

I closed my eyes when I felt the jolt. I stayed that way, hoping to hear Sebastian's voice. All I heard at first was a gentle rustling of leaves in the breeze, followed a moment later by the sound of the front door.

"Hey," Rory asked, "where'd that tree come from?"

Tree? I opened my eyes. Oh, gosh. I'd done it again.

Right at the edge of the lawn where Sebastian had been standing, I saw a small tree.

"Where'd it come from?" Rory asked again.

"I got it at the mall," I told him. "But I don't like it here—it's the wrong size. I think I'll return it."

He nodded, as if this made sense. Then he reached past me and pulled off a small leaf.

"Rory, you'll hurt him!"

He shook his head. "It's just a tree."

"It's a living thing."

He stared at the leaf in his hand. "I can get some glue."

"That's okay. One leaf won't make any difference."
I hoped I was right.

Rory shrugged and dropped the leaf on the ground. Then he wandered off.

"Would you like a snack?"

I looked up at the front door. Mom was there. She hadn't noticed there was a new tree growing in the yard. I think people see a lot less when they get older—especially when they become parents. "Maybe later," I told her. "I'm not hungry right now."

"Okay." She went back inside.

"Hey, is Splat around? He just went running out of my house. He kept shouting, 'I'll get her for this' "

I spun toward the sidewalk, and found myself facing Norman again. "I think he was headed back toward your house," I told him.

He nodded and started to go away. After two steps, he turned back and said, "Nice tree. It's a thornless

honey locust, *Gleditsia triacanthos*, if I recall correctly. You might want to prune some of the lower branches."

"I might." I watched him walk off. Norman saw everything, but he noticed very little.

As soon as Norman was gone, I grabbed a branch of the tree. Since I'd shouted *no* to make it happen, this time I shouted, "On!"

Sure enough, the tree changed back into my brother.

"Ouch!" Sebastian shouted, reaching up to the side of his head. "Why'd you pull my hair?"

I glanced down at the leaf Rory had dropped. It wasn't a leaf anymore, but a clump of hair. "It was an accident," I said, stepping on top of the hair so Sebastian wouldn't see it.

"You did it again, didn't you?" Sebastian said. He was starting to turn red. "You did something before, and you just did it again. What did you do?"

I didn't have the energy to keep hiding this from him. "I don't know," I told him. "But whatever happened, it only seems to happen when you tease me."

"I don't tease you," he said.

"Yes, you do."

"Do not. You're the one who's always bugging me. You can be such a pain. Do you know that?" He poked me with his finger.

"And you—" I almost poked him back. Instead, I moved away and held my hands up. "Trust me—you don't want to continue this."

"You've got that right." He stormed off, leaving me

to wonder how things had gotten out of control so quickly.

I went up to my room and read until it was time for dinner. At first, I tried making notes about anything that seemed important. After a while, I realized that there was no single answer to anything. Power seemed to take many forms. Some witches cast spells with words; others used objects. Some had amazing abilities; others could do little more than make fresh milk turn sour or get rid of warts.

There was some scary stuff, too. People used to think there were witches all around. They believed a witch would float, so when they thought someone was a witch, they'd throw her into a lake. If she floated, that proved she was a witch, so they'd kill her. If she sank and drowned, they knew she wasn't a witch. I felt terrible when I thought about how many innocent people had gone through a trial they couldn't win.

I had no idea what sort of limits there were to my own power. I pointed at a bottle of perfume on my dresser. "Rise," I said.

I didn't expect anything to happen. *Wrong again,* I thought, as something unexpected happened.

Fifteen

FAMILY TIME

The bottle turned into a fish.

Yuck.

It flopped around on my dresser like—well, like a fish. I saw a black flash as Darling leaped up and grabbed it.

"Let it go!" I shouted.

Darling ignored me and dragged the fish under my bed. Ewww . . .

"Dinner," Mom called from downstairs.

I walked out of the room, eager to get away from the sounds of Darling tearing into the fish. I didn't eat red meat. I used to eat fish, but after what I'd just seen, I might cross that off my list, too.

I joined Mom, Sebastian, and Rory in the kitchen.

"We're having spaghetti," Mom said.

"With meat sauce?" Sebastian asked, grinning at me with a look that told me he'd get even any way he could.

Mom pointed to a pot on the stove. "The sauce is separate."

"Thanks." I helped set the table, then got butter from the fridge for my spaghetti.

Sebastian picked up the pot of sauce. "Mooooo," he said, waving it at me. "Poor little cow goes mooooo." He put the pot down, lifted the lid, and looked inside. "Oops, can't go mooooo anymore. Got ground up. Nothing in here but mini-moos."

"Moooooooo," Rory said. "Minimoooooooo."

If Dad were here, he would have stopped Sebastian, but Mom went a lot easier on him.

"That reminds me," Sebastian said. He opened the fridge and grabbed a carton of milk. "Moooo," he said again as he poured a glass. "Liquid moooo." He grinned at me and took a big gulp.

I glared at him.

"*Yecchhhh!*" he shouted, spitting the mouthful of milk on the floor.

"Sebastian!" Mom shouted.

"It's sour," he said after he'd wiped his mouth on his sleeve.

"Let me try," Rory said, running over to him.

"Oh, man," Sebastian said. "You don't want to try this." He went to the sink and stuck his mouth under the faucet. Then he looked at the carton. "Buttermilk? Oh, man, that was awful."

"Buttermilk?" Mom said. "I must have picked up the wrong carton at the market. I'm sorry."

"What a shame," I said as my smile stretched into a grin. Whether it was a happy accident or a jolt from my witchy power, it seemed like a wonderful punishment. "But you should like buttermilk," I told Sebastian. "It's from cows. Mmmmmm, mmmmm, mmmmoooooo."

"Just shut up," he said.

"Certainly." I didn't say another word about it, but I did giggle once or twice while I ate, and I sipped my juice with great delight.

After we'd cleaned up from dinner, we got a call from Dad. I talked with him when Mom and Rory were done.

"Hi," I told him. "I miss you."

"I know, Angel, but I'll be home Wednesday. And I sent you a surprise. It should be there tomorrow."

Dad calls me *Angel* sometimes, but he tries not to do it when anyone else is listening since I'm getting older. But I don't mind. It makes me feel special. We talked for another minute; then Sebastian grabbed the phone. I stepped away from him before anything could happen.

As I was walking out of the kitchen, the doorbell rang.

"I got it," I called. I ran to the front door and opened it.

The woman—the beautiful one from the spell shop—was standing on the porch. "There's been a mistake," she said. "You have something that belongs to me."

Sixteen

DINGDONG

Something that belongs to her? I remembered the words I'd read: *Power seeks its rightful owner.* In a flash of quick thinking, I managed to mutter, "I . . . uh . . . ummm . . . what?"

She smiled. "Relax, child. It was a simple error. She'd promised it to me and then she gave it to you. But this should make things fair."

She held up a twenty-dollar bill. Was that all my power was worth? I shook my head. "No."

"All right," she said. She reached into her pocket and pulled out another twenty-dollar bill. "Surely this is enough."

"You can't put a price on it," I told her.

"But it's just a book," she said.

"A book?" I was too relieved to protest. "I'll be right back." As I ran up to my room, I wondered how the woman had found me. Then I remembered that Jan had used my last name at the spell shop. We were the only Claypool family in the Lewington phone book. I came back down and handed the book to the woman. She gave me the money.

"Such lovely hair," she said. She reached out and stroked my hair where it brushed my shoulder, then turned and walked off.

I put the money in my pocket and went up to my room. Forty dollars for a book that hadn't cost me anything—something wasn't right. Before I could think things through, the doorbell rang again.

"Angie," Mom called, "one of your friends is here to see you."

I ran down the stairs, then skidded to a halt. Never in a million years, except maybe in a million nightmares, would I ever have expected to find May Mellon at my door.

"Uh, hi?" I said. I almost added: *Did you change your mind and decide you wanted to beat me up after all?*

She jerked her head to the side. For an instant, I thought it was some kind of dreadful twitch. Then I realized she wanted me to come out to the porch. I walked through the doorway, feeling vulnerable. May was big and strong. She was powerful enough to pick me up and throw me off the porch. But I had power, too. That thought made me stand a bit straighter and look her in the eye. "What do you want?"

"Does this match?" she asked.

86

"What?" I had no idea what she was talking about.

"Does it match!" she shouted, as if my problem had to do with the volume of her words and not the meaning. "You're supposed to know this stuff." She pointed at her shirt.

"Oh, your clothes." Amazing. A few hours ago, she was ready to smash me. Now she wanted my advice. I tried not to flinch as I studied her outfit: jeans, a red belt, and a green shirt with orange flowers on it. "You look fine." What could I do? I couldn't tell her she looked like a walking advertisement for Hawaiian Christmas vacations. She'd clobber me for sure.

May nodded, grunted a word that might have been "Thanks," and walked down the steps. I should have made my escape, but something didn't seem right. Why was she wondering about her clothes on a Sunday evening?

"May . . . ," I called after her.

She turned back.

"Do you have a date or something?"

May grinned. "Lance Anderson said that Danny Gleason wanted to buy me a soda at the Burger Pit. I'm supposed to meet him out front by the big plastic burger." She turned and lumbered off.

Oh, no. I was sure Lance was playing a joke on her. Danny was the cutest boy in the school, and he hung out with the cool crowd. Lance hung with the mean crowd. I wanted to warn May, but I knew she'd never believe me. I went to the living room and sat down.

The second my rear hit the chair, the doorbell rang. It was Miss Chutney. "I came to warn you," she said. "I believe Elestra is a power-seeker."

"Who?" I asked.

"Elestra Malacorsa. The instant she saw you in my shop, she knew what you carried. To those who know how to look for power, someone like you shines with the brightness of a star. That's why I made you leave. And that's why I gave you the book. You need to know as much as possible about your power. You are in great danger from her."

"She was just here," I said. "But she didn't try to hurt me. She paid me for the book." I pulled the bills from my pocket and handed them to Miss Chutney. "I guess this is yours."

She thrust the money back at me. "I don't want anything of hers." She rubbed her hands together, as she had in her shop.

"I don't understand any of this," I said. "I never asked for power. And now that I have it, I don't know how to use it."

"Be patient. The power must find its own path." She paused, then softly added, "Poor Lucinda. I'll miss her."

"Was that the woman who gave me the power?"

Miss Chutney nodded. "We were old friends." She took a step back and looked at me. "What I wouldn't give for such a gift." She rubbed her hands together again.

"You don't have any power?"

She shook her head. "No. I've been close to it, and studied it all my life, but that is all. I would gladly take it if it were given to me."

I looked at this kindly old woman as she made those odd gestures with her hands, and suddenly wondered whether I could trust her. Maybe she was the one who wanted my power. "Thanks for telling me all this," I said. I put my hand on the door.

"Be careful. Elestra is dangerous."

"I'll be careful." I closed the door. But I didn't walk away. After such a steady stream of visitors, I figured I'd wait to see if there were more. Sure enough, less than a minute later, the doorbell rang.

"My, you're popular tonight," Mom called from the kitchen.

"School project," I called back. I opened the door.

It was Katrina.

"Hi," I said.

She stared down at her feet. Finally, she looked up and said, "I never thanked you for the other day. I think you saved me. Twice. So thanks."

"Sure. You're welcome." I stood there, not really knowing what else to say.

"Mewrrrr." Darling came down the steps and joined us.

"I named her Darling," I said. "I got the idea from you. So I guess I should thank you, too."

Katrina knelt and petted my cat. Then she stood up and said, "Thanks again."

"Sure." As I watched Katrina walk away, I thought about the way she'd rushed toward the park yesterday. Was she the one who should have gotten the power?

I went to my room and put the money from Elestra on my dresser. I still felt funny about keeping it. I knew what Jan would do—she'd run right out and give it to charity. Maybe I'd do that tomorrow. Or maybe I'd spend it on myself.

I sat on my bed and tried to use my power. I rubbed my hands the way I'd seen Miss Chutney rub hers. As I did that, a breeze began to blow through the room. The bills on my dresser fluttered like two birds. Maybe Miss Chutney had lied when she'd told me she didn't have any power.

I waved my hands in different patterns. Once, when I opened my hand quickly, my closet door flew open. Then, when I clenched my fist, the door slammed shut. I tried to make the door move just by thinking about it. It shook a little, but that was all.

After an hour of experimenting, I was exhausted. Power didn't come without effort. I got dressed for bed and turned out the light. Darling crawled onto my legs and settled down.

"Good night, Darling," I said quietly.

"Mereww."

I started to drift off.

The hissing woke me.

Seventeen

BAD MONEY

I sat up and looked around.

For a moment, I didn't notice anything unusual. Then I heard the hissing again, like the sound of acid eating through metal. It was coming from my dresser. I flipped on my lamp. Instead of chasing away the terrors of the night, my light revealed them.

The money changed before my eyes. A snake head, filled with dripping fangs and topped with sharp horns, had already grown on each bill. The rest of the bill swelled into a body. Green legs sprouted from the sides. Black claws sprang from the toes.

I wanted to close my eyes and scream, but I knew that if I closed my eyes, I might never open them again. Somewhere inside me, I found the courage to face those monsters.

Darling started to leap at them, but I grabbed her.

The creatures looked bigger than she could handle. They crawled toward the front of the dresser. Wings sprouted from the sides of the swollen bodies.

The creatures perched on the edge of the dresser, moving their heads rapidly as if searching for prey. Their tongues slithered in and out, tasting the air. Then, both at the same time, they stared at me and raised their wings. They were ready to leap. I put Darling back on the bed, then held up my fists. This had to work. I focused my attention on the dresser and flung open my fingers. The top drawer flew open so violently that the whole dresser tipped forward. Screaming in frustration, scrambling wildly to hold on, the creatures slid off the edge of the dresser and toppled into the drawer.

Shut, I thought as I closed my fingers, but my concentration was broken by the hissing screams coming from the drawer. I squeezed my fists so hard, I could feel my nails digging into my palms. The drawer stayed open. I tried again. Nothing happened. I could see the creatures trying to climb out.

I leaped from the bed and ran across the room. I slammed the drawer shut and pushed against it with both hands. I heard thumps and crashes against the wood, and felt a series of jolts as the creatures tried to escape. The wood of the drawer started to crack.

I held on. The thumps grew weaker. These creatures weren't natural. I hoped they couldn't last long. Whatever they were—they'd been created to do their job quickly. I shuddered as I looked at the claw marks

on top of the dresser and thought about what that job was.

I nearly pulled my hands away as I felt a sudden blast of heat. Then everything became quiet.

I was pushing against the dresser so hard that I'd tipped it back toward the wall. My arms and shoulders ached from the effort. Slowly, I stepped away, then reached forward and slid the drawer open an inch.

Silence.

I opened it another inch and looked inside, ready to slam it shut at the first sign of movement.

Two small piles of green dust sat inside, on top of my jewelry box. I took the box out of the drawer and put it on my bed. Darling bent over to sniff at the remains of the creatures. She sneezed, and the dust vanished in a cloud.

"Elestra," I whispered. She'd given me the money. What would those creatures have done to me if I hadn't stopped them?

I stared at the spots where the dust had been. I don't think I would have moved for a long time, but the shattering blast of a train whistle ripped through the room.

Eighteen

POWER AND FURY

I crossed the room and stared at the source of the sound. The mirror on the dresser was fogged. I wiped it with my hand, but the fog remained. It wasn't on the mirror— it was *in* the mirror. For an instant, deep within the fog, I saw a large, heavy shape. A train. It crashed into a smaller object. The scene died too quickly for me to tell what was happening. But the sight left me trembling.

"Too much," I said to Darling as I backed away from the dresser and collapsed on my bed. In seconds, I was asleep.

I felt better in the morning. A ripple of nervousness still gripped my insides, but I felt stronger, too. Sebastian was at the kitchen counter when I went down.

"You still angry?" I asked.

He looked over his shoulder and grinned. "How could I stay mad at my own sister?"

"You sure?"

He nodded.

"Can I ask you something?" I figured he was such a big fan of monsters and horror movies that he might know some useful stuff.

"Anything, dear sister," he said.

"Thanks, I need to ask you—"

"But first, how about a nice crisp piece of bacon?" As he said that, he whirled and shoved a plate full of fried pig pieces under my nose.

"Quit it." I pushed his arm away.

Shock.

Sebastian dropped to the floor, turning into a puddle of slimy stuff that looked like spilled oatmeal. True to his nickname, he landed with a *splat*. The plate hung in the air for an instant. I grabbed it before it could fall. Then I stared down at my slimy brother.

"Giving meat another chance?" Mom asked as she walked into the kitchen.

"Uh, no," I said, putting down the plate.

"Oh, dear," Mom said, glancing at the floor. Then, with that amazing acrobatic ability that moms have, she reached out and snatched a handful of paper towels, stooped and wiped up Sebastian, and tossed the towels into the garbage can.

"Oh, good grief . . ."

Mom gave me a puzzled look as she left the kitchen. An instant later, Rory came running in from the living room, carrying his half-empty bowl.

96

"I'm full," he said, dumping the rest of the milk and soggy cereal into the garbage can.

He ran out of the kitchen.

I hurried over to the garbage can and stared at the gooey mess. When he'd changed, I'd said, "Quit it." I needed to reverse it. But I wasn't sure how to say "quit" backward. I tried, "Tiqua tih."

Nothing happened.

"Tikwa tih," I said, starting to feel a tingle of worry. Nothing.

"Tikuua tih . . ."

No change. I wondered whether I should scoop Sebastian up and put him in a safe place. Did he need to be refrigerated? This was crazy. I took a deep breath and tried to think calmly. Okay, I asked myself, why wasn't it working? I'd reversed the words. But I'd only reversed each word by itself—maybe I also needed to reverse the order of the words. "Okay, this will work," I said. I took a deep breath. "Tih tikwa."

"Hey!"

Sebastian was standing in the garbage can. Cereal and milk dripped down his face.

He opened his mouth. He pointed at me, his finger trembling with anger. "You—!"

This didn't look like a good time for a deep discussion of the lore and myths of witchcraft. I grabbed the roll of paper towels and handed it to him. "Here, clean yourself up before Mom sees what a mess you made."

I snatched a banana for breakfast, got my backpack,

and headed to school. When I reached the front lawn of the building, I walked past Lance Anderson and his gang. They were laughing about something. I had a good idea what it was.

"Bet she waited there for hours," Lance said.

I glared at them, wishing that Lance could feel as bad as May. To him, it was nothing but a joke. To her, it was probably a painful memory that might never heal completely.

The bell rang. Everyone headed toward the building. I glared at Lance. The wind whipped around me, raising a cloud of dust.

No, I thought, realizing I'd unleashed something.

Nineteen

GLUB

A piece of notebook paper, blown by the wind, flew up at Lance's face. He raised a hand to catch it.

I breathed a sigh of relief. A piece of paper couldn't do any damage.

As Lance reached out, he tripped on a crack in the sidewalk and went tumbling. A crowd formed around him. Then someone went for the nurse. I hovered at the edge of the mob. Lance was holding his wrist and moaning. The nurse looked at it and said, "It might be broken."

I rushed to my homeroom.

"I think I broke Lance's arm," I told Jan after I'd plunked down in the seat next to her.

Jan shrugged. "Somebody had to."

A moment later, May came in. I could almost feel the fury rising from her. As she walked to her desk in the last row, she flicked her hand out and hit Billy Winkdale on the back of the head. It wasn't a hard hit—it was more like a high five. Then she slammed her books on her desk and glared around the room as if daring anyone to get in her way.

"She's in a great mood," Jan said.

"It's not all her fault," I said. Then I told Jan what Lance had done.

"Nasty trick," Jan said.

"But she's pretty nasty herself."

"Maybe she was nicer when she was younger," Jan said.

I wondered whether people had played a lot of mean tricks on May. But why were those people nasty themselves? Where did it begin? Just thinking about it made my head hurt.

"I think the rain forest is too big a place to start with," Jan said, breaking into my thoughts.

"What?"

"You have to start smaller," Jan said. "Maybe you could help the dolphins first. Or how about the speckled lake owl? It's still endangered, right?"

"I can't fool around with this, Jan," I told her. "I don't want to hurt anyone else."

"So maybe you should start out real slow, like with those hot-fudge sundaes."

Morning announcements began, so Jan and I had to stop talking. Then we went outside for the bus to the high school, where we took our swim classes.

When we got there, we put on our swimsuits and lined up along one side of the pool.

"Everybody in the water!" Ms. Rambowski yelled. She blew her whistle and we all jumped in.

I guess I was somewhere in the middle of my leap when it sank in on me that I might not sink. I hit the water and started to bob on the surface like my suit was filled with air. Around me, the rest of the class had started to tread water.

"Jan," I whispered, reaching out to tap her shoulder. It was hard to do anything the way I was floating.

"Oh, boy," she gasped when she saw me. Or maybe she said, "Oh, buoy." I really wasn't in any position to tell.

We both glanced around. Nobody else had noticed me yet, but I knew someone would look my way any second. Ms. Rambowski was standing right behind me.

Jan took two strong strokes toward the center of the pool. Then she screamed and vanished under the water. An instant later, she popped back up, yelled, "Help!" and sank back down again. Ms. Rambowski leaped over me, diving into the water.

I almost went to save Jan before I realized what she was doing. What a great friend she was. I climbed out of the water. A moment later, Ms. Rambowski dragged Jan to the side of the pool.

Gasping and sputtering, Jan choked out the word, "Cramp," and then started coughing.

"I'll stay with her," I said, rushing over to her side.

"Would you?" Ms. Rambowski asked. "That would be so kind."

"I'd be happy to," I said. I helped Jan leave the pool.

"How was I?" she asked when we got to the locker room.

"Amazing," I said. "I was ready to rescue you myself."

"Thanks. What exactly was going on back there?"

"I'm a witch," I told her. "It's as simple as that."

"You can be a crab, maybe," Jan said. "And a bit of a grump once in a while. But I wouldn't call you a witch. Except for that time when your mom wouldn't let you go to the Twisting Apes concert. Then you were a real witch."

"I'm serious. That's what all this power is about. I can't cross running water. And I float."

Jan nodded. "If that's the case, I can see where you might want to avoid swimming pools. But you know, it would have been fun if we'd stayed. We could have stuck an umbrella in your belly button and used you to hold cans of soda."

She laughed. Then I started to laugh, and both of us had to struggle to keep from being heard out in the pool.

"What am I going to do?" I asked Jan.

"The backstroke?"

We barely managed to look properly serious again by the time the class returned to the locker room.

When we got back to school, it was time for history. As I walked into the room, I saw that we had a substitute. She was standing at the desk with her head down, studying the lesson plan. Then she looked up and I saw her face. My arms dropped to my sides, and I heard my books hit the floor with a crash.

Twenty

TEACHER'S PET

Elestra Malacorsa smiled at me. "Hello," she said to the class. "I'm Miss Malacorsa. I'll be your substitute for the next few days. It seems that poor Mr. Whittledown was taken suddenly ill. From what I understand, he ate a piece of bad fruit. But I'm sure you'll all work just as hard for me."

During the class, she acted like we'd never met. When the bell rang, I had a hard time gathering my books. They kept slipping from my hands. When I finally got them, I looked up and saw I was the only one in the room with Elestra.

"You are in great danger," she said.

"Yeah, from you." I took a step toward the door, wondering if it would do any good to run.

"I'm not a threat. I'm here to help you. As your power struggles to take form, anything might happen."

Maybe she was trying to help me. But there was something I needed to know before I could decide whether to trust her. "Why did you buy the book?"

"To protect you. The woman from the shop is a power-seeker. I suspect she has some of her own, but she wants more. It's lucky for you I came into her shop and saw what she was doing. She's the sly sort. Lying on the floor, looking so helpless, I'm sure she was planning something nasty. I was afraid that there was danger in the book. Traps can take many forms. I'm sorry I had to deceive you, but it was the best way."

"But the money attacked me." I shuddered as I thought about the creatures on my dresser.

She frowned. "And you thought that was my doing?"

"Yes. I mean, I did think that. I guess I made it happen myself." *Or did I?* I remembered that Miss Chutney had held the money and then made those motions with her hands.

"You see? You're in danger until you can control your power. Until then, I'll be here to help protect you."

The bell rang for the next class. "I have to go."

I rushed into science and took my seat. If Elestra was really here to help me, that would be a great relief. I wondered how long it would take to learn to control my power. Maybe it didn't matter. Soon, if I wanted to, I could pass my power to someone else. But who? I looked around. Katrina, at the far corner of the room, caught my glance and looked back for an instant, then quickly turned her head away. If ever there was a person who could use some power, it was Katrina.

Across the room, I saw May carving away at the top of her desk with a pen. If ever there was someone who already had too much power, it was May Mellon. But in some ways, she didn't have any power at all. She could push the rest of us around, but people didn't like being pushed around. I didn't care to think what someone like her would do with my power.

"Well, Angelina? I'm waiting for your answer."

I looked up at Mrs. Pushbind. I'd been so deep in thought, I didn't have a clue what she'd asked me. *Give me a break*, I thought. *Just ask someone else.* I blew a puff of air up at my bangs in frustration.

Mrs. Pushbind blinked, then said, "Well, never mind, I'll just ask someone else." She walked across the room and repeated the question.

I felt my whole body tingle. If I had just done what I thought I'd done, I had awesome power. I watched the teacher and tried to make her do something else. *Bark like a dog*, I thought. For good measure, I puffed up at my bangs again. She cleared her throat. It sounded a little like a bark, but I wasn't sure I'd caused it. I looked over at May. *Scratch your head*, I thought as I puffed air.

May scratched her head.

But that wasn't a real test. May was always scratching.

"Clear your desks," Mrs. Pushbind said. "It's time for a quiz." She started writing the questions on the board.

Around me, everyone was hard at work, scribbling

away. I thought about what I'd read in the books I'd borrowed. It helped to have an object to focus the power. That was one of the keys. Lance had been hurt because I'd just let the power loose without any direction. I wouldn't do that again. But I had to find out whether I could control my power.

I held up my own pencil and broke the tip with my thumb. *Snap*. Then I blew on the tip. Energy flowed from me into the air, spreading in all directions. *Snap, snap, snap*. Two dozen other pencil tips snapped. I couldn't help grinning as the whole class headed for the pencil sharpener. I noticed that my thumb was a bit sore, as if I'd actually used it to break every single one of those pencils.

Mrs. Pushbind looked like she wanted to say something, but all the kids held up their pencils to show her.

"I did it," I whispered to Jan as I got in line behind her.

"What was the point?" she whispered back.

I realized she was making a joke about the pencil points. But I still answered her. "The point is power," I said.

Life at school was about to get very exciting.

Twenty-one

PRANKS A LOT

I didn't break the pencils again. I felt that I wouldn't learn anything by repeating myself. As I walked down the hall with Jan on our way toward lunch, I thought about what else I could do. The cafeteria was loaded with possibilities.

"Lunch is going to be interesting," I told Jan as we took our seats. We always brought sandwiches so we wouldn't have to stand in line.

"Hardly the word I'd choose." Jan peeked into her bag and said, "Nope. Nothing interesting in here. Nothing edible in here, for that matter."

We sat at an empty table. I didn't want anyone to notice what I was doing. I looked over at the noisiest table. A bunch of kids were laughing and shouting and horsing around. Kenny Volst was standing up, leaning on the edge of the table, saying something to Mike

Howardson. I took a drinking straw and balanced it on one end. *Slip*, I said to myself. I blew a puff of air, knocking over the straw. Kenny's hands slipped and he fell face-first into his plate of food. Lunch today was what the cafeteria people called Hungarian goulash, but it was really just noodles with red sauce and chunks of mystery meat. It looked great on Kenny.

Jan stared at Kenny, then back at me. "Was that you—?"

"Yup." I tried to turn everyone's milk sour. But nothing happened. Only about half the things I tried actually worked. I did manage to make Cody Perez spill juice all over his pants. And I got Melissa Canutti to burp real loudly. Three times! She looked around like she couldn't believe what had come out of her mouth. All her stuck-up friends got very embarrassed.

"One favor," Jan said after Melissa's third ear-shattering belch.

"What?"

"Just don't do anything like that at the other end. Okay?"

"Jan! I'd never stoop so low." As soon as the words left my mouth, I started laughing.

Jan was laughing, too. Then her face lit up like she was suddenly struck with a great idea. "Why don't you cast a spell on *him*," she whispered, pointing past me.

I glanced over my shoulder. Danny Gleason was at the table right behind me.

"I couldn't," I whispered back.

"Sure you could," Jan said.

Why not? Trying not to giggle or attract attention, I got out my notebook and drew a heart on a piece of paper. Then I tore the heart into tiny pieces and gathered them in my hand. I was pleased that I was getting so good at using the power.

I turned and puffed the pieces of paper toward Danny.

"Watch out. Coming through!"

"Make way!"

I jerked back as someone ran between me and Danny. Then I cringed as all my fragments of heart scattered across my two worst nightmares—Clem and Clyde Mellon.

If ever I'd hoped to fail at something, now was the time. I held my breath—my magical, powerful, witchy breath.

Twenty-two

HOW DO YOU DO THAT?

Clem and Clyde stopped running and stared at me as if they were watching a sunrise over a mountain lake or a rare flower blooming.

"You sure are pretty," Clem said.

"Saw her first," Clyde said. He pushed Clem.

"Did not," Clem said. "I saw her first." He pushed back.

Clyde took a swing at Clem. Clem ducked and tackled Clyde. They went flying like a sack full of melons, punching and shouting and hitting. Another hulk rumbled past me as May dived in, yelling, "Break it up, you two!" In an instant, she was hauling them apart, clutching each by an ear.

"I'm not hungry anymore," I said to Jan. Part of me felt guilty about pulling these stunts, but I had to admit, except for the part with Clem and Clyde, I was having fun. And then I felt guilty for enjoying myself.

As I left the cafeteria, exhaustion dropped on me like a mountain of rocks. I staggered, then leaned against a wall.

"What's wrong?" Jan asked.

"I'm tired," I said. I felt better after a moment, but I realized it took a lot of energy to use my power. I held back from doing anything else for the rest of the school day, and I made sure I avoided Clem and Clyde whenever I walked through the halls.

I went with Jan to her house after school. "So, what's it like?" she asked when we got to her room. "I mean, how do you do it?"

I'd been trying to figure it all out myself. "It's sort of like imagining. I have to pretend that what I want to happen is already real. But it's also like wishing." I looked around for something to use as an example.

"Sounds kind of like daydreaming," Jan said.

"Yeah. That's not a bad description." I went to Jan's dresser and got a white handkerchief. I held it and imagined that it was green.

"Wow," Jan said as the handkerchief changed color. "Can you change it back?"

"I don't know." I tried, but it didn't work. "Hey," I said as I thought of a good way to explain it. "Remember when my dad took us bowling?"

"Yeah. How could I forget?" Jan grinned. "I kept

throwing the ball into the next alley. What's that got to do with this?"

"Near the beginning, I threw the ball perfectly once. I knocked all the pins down. I thought—hey, *this is easy.* But as soon as I tried to do it again, I couldn't."

"Yeah." Jan snapped her fingers. "That happened to me with tennis. I hit a great shot, and as soon as I try to do it again, I can't. But with your power, if you think about something the right way, you can do anything, right?"

I shook my head. "Just small stuff. Big stuff is harder. I need to use something to help my mind focus." I got up and faced the bed. I imagined the bed rising, and at the same time I lifted the handkerchief.

"Hey!" Jan shouted as her bed started to rise.

As the bed rose an inch from the floor, I could feel myself getting tired. I relaxed and the bed fell with a crash.

A moment later, Jan's phone rang. She picked it up and said, "Sorry." Then she hung it up and told me, "My dad says to keep the noise down. He's thinking about the universe and needs peace and quiet."

She was the only person I knew who got phone calls from her folks when they were all in the same house. "Sorry." I dropped the handkerchief. "There's more, but I haven't really figured it all out. Words seem to have some kind of power. I mean, they can help me focus, but they seem to have more use than just that. I wish I was better with words."

We talked awhile longer; then I went back to my place and got started on my homework. I couldn't resist trying to do it the easy way. I managed to make all the math answers appear, but that didn't save me any work, since I had to check everything to make sure it was right. Then I tried to create an essay for English class. But when I read it, I wondered whether it had come from somewhere. What if it was a famous essay? I'd get in trouble for copying. In the end, I wrote my own essay.

Nothing unusual happened until that evening when I walked into the living room. "Can you help me clean up?" Mom asked. She was in the middle of one of her assaults on dirt and disorder. The furniture had been moved out so she could get to the whole floor, and the windows were wide open, allowing a breeze to blow through the room.

"Sure. What do you want me to do?"

She pointed to the closet. "I spilled some dirt when I was repotting those plants. Could you get the electric broom and sweep it up? I need to go fold the laundry."

"Okay." I went to the closet. The electric broom is like an upright vacuum. As I grabbed the handle, it tugged against my grip. I probably should have let go. But I held on.

Twenty-three

SWEEPING THE SKY

The broom shot out of the closet, dragging me across the floor. "Hey!" I shouted.

The front of the broom lifted into the air and headed toward the window. I tried to stop, but I just kept sliding along. Mom had done a nice job waxing the floors. By the time we reached the window, I was nearly off my feet.

The broom flew outside, zooming up like a jet taking off from an airport. Then the front flipped back between my legs, and I was riding it.

I tried to make it turn back to the house, but it didn't pay any attention to me. This wasn't a spell I'd cast—this was the power running wild. I wasn't in control. We—the broom and I—climbed higher, soaring in an upward spiral.

The air grew cooler as we rose. We slowed, and we

were no longer alone. Birds flew toward us from all directions. Crows, wrens, sparrows, and cardinals sped across the sky. A red-tailed hawk joined us. It was beautiful.

I was in my element—I was in the air.

We flew far above Lewington. I tried to spot my house. I found the school. The track was a tiny oval far below. The breeze whipped my hair as I traced the streets back to my house.

I stopped clutching the broom and just held on lightly to the handle. I didn't think I'd fall, even if I let go. I relaxed and enjoyed the ride, scanning the ground for more places I knew. The park was easy to spot—a large rectangle of green plunked near the houses and streets. And across from it, sure enough, the mall really did look like a giant turtle, its five corridors stretching from the Hub like arms, legs, and a head.

After circling the whole town, the broom swooped sharply downward, leaving the birds behind. We picked up speed as we got closer to the house. Air blasted past me, rippling my shirt and tugging my hair. It felt fabulous. By the time we reached the living room window, we were going so fast, I could hear a *whoosh*. We shot into the room and turned in a tight circle, zooming around so rapidly that the breeze pulled up all the dirt. The circle grew tighter and tighter, until we were spinning like an ice skater in the middle of the room.

We stopped.

The cyclone of dirt spun away from us, then danced across the room, up the wall, and out the window.

Wow.

"Hey, good job. Looks like you got all the dirt," Mom said as she walked into the room.

"Thanks." I waited a moment to steady myself, then carried the broom back to the closet. My head was still in the clouds; my feet were still a mile above the earth.

Things started to get a little wild in my room again that night. Mostly, the stuff on my dresser and in my closet began shifting around. But I stood there and said, "No!" and concentrated on keeping the power under control. It worked. It sort of reminded me of when Dad fixes a dripping faucet. At first, there's water leaking out where it isn't supposed to. Then Dad tightens something and makes it better.

While I was thinking about Dad and the faucet, I glimpsed a train in the mirror again. The sight of the train, all wrapped in fog, and the scream of the whistle, shook me pretty badly.

As I was falling asleep, I heard this horrible screeching noise. At first, I thought it was another burst of uncontrolled power. "Sounds like a cat fight," I said to Darling as I looked out the window.

It was much worse than that. Clem—who I could tell from Clyde because he had shorter hair— was under my window. I think he was singing to me, but it was hard to tell. Before I could yell at him to leave, Clyde showed up.

"Get out," Clem said. "I was here first."

"You stole my idea," Clyde said. He grabbed his

brother and they started wrestling. The fight carried them down the street and away from my house.

That night, I dreamed of birds and brooms. But someone kept throwing melons at me.

In the morning, when I went down for breakfast, I saw a box on the table with my name on it. "The package from your father arrived," Mom said.

"Where's Sebastian?" I asked, noticing that my brother had already opened his box.

Mom shrugged. "He left early. First time I ever saw that boy eager to get to school."

I suspected his eagerness had to do with avoiding me.

"Look at mine," Rory said. He held up his gift—a plastic bird with wings that flapped. Rory wound it up and let go. It flew across the kitchen. Rory laughed and chased after it.

I tore open my package and lifted out a bracelet made of woven strips of colored paper. "It's beautiful!" I couldn't wait to show it to Jan. I grabbed a quick breakfast, then headed off toward school.

When I got there, I saw Clyde Mellon standing by the front entrance, holding a bouquet of flowers. His hair was combed, he was wearing a clean shirt, and his eyes had the look that reminded me of the puppies in the pet shop. I could tell it was Clyde because he had all his front teeth.

I shuddered and sneaked around toward the side door. Clem was waiting there with a huge box of chocolates and a grin like a piano keyboard. I slunk to the back of the school and started to climb in an open window. As soon as possible, I had to find a way to remove my spell.

"Need help?"

I looked up. Elestra reached out and gave me a hand into the room. "You seem to have some admirers," she said. Then she glanced at my wrist. "A gift from one of them?"

I shook my head and hurried off to homeroom. When the bell rang for first period, I checked the halls carefully for lovestruck Mellons before going to English class.

Everyone groaned when Ms. Sudo told us we'd be writing poems. I really stink at poetry. I started to write:

I got a new bracelet,
It's paper, not silver
I like it a lot,
But

That's where I got stuck. I tried to cast a spell to find a rhyme. Nothing happened. I drew a circle around the word *silver*, hoping that might help. It didn't. I blew on the paper. Even that didn't get me a rhyme. I couldn't understand why my power wasn't working.

"Angelina," Ms. Sudo said, looking down at my paper.

"Yes?"

"You might want to start over. Nothing rhymes with *silver*."

"Really?"

She nodded, then told me another word that had no rhymes, so I wouldn't use it, either.

"Thanks." I started again. By the end of the period, I'd produced a really bad poem. But at least it all rhymed.

As we handed in our papers, a motion outside the window caught my eye. Miss Chutney was standing in the yard, staring at me. Just then, I felt a burning on my wrist. I looked down at my bracelet. It was no longer paper. It looked like iron now. Sharp barbs grew out of the metal, stabbing into my skin.

Twenty-four

TRAPS AND TREACHERY

The bell rang. I grabbed my wrist and ran from the classroom. Beneath my fingers, the bracelet squirmed like a living creature. I yanked, but it stung me with a million painful pincers. All around me, kids were rushing to their next class.

I clamped my jaw down to keep from screaming and pulled harder at the bracelet. It wouldn't break. My wrist felt as if it were wrapped with burning coals.

I knew my only chance was to stay calm. But I could barely fight down the panic. *Paper!* my mind screamed. *What beats paper?* In the game, scissors beats paper. But this was no game.

Earth, air, fire, and water. I was air, but air was no use. *Water beats paper!*

Hoping this was true even when the paper seemed like iron, I raced down the hall to the water fountain and held my wrist under the cool flow. As the first spray hit, I could feel the bracelet shiver and go slack. I yanked and it came free. The broken ends jerked like a crushed caterpillar, then flopped loosely in my hand. An instant later, the whole thing melted into a muddy mess that sifted through my fingers like damp beach sand.

My skin still stung, but the pain was fading.

Miss Chutney. She'd done this to me. And she was somewhere nearby. I wasn't afraid anymore. I was angry. *Watch out, lady. I'm coming.* I stormed out the door and down the steps.

"Where are you?" I called.

I ran around the side of the building and spotted her behind the school. "You!" I shouted. As I pointed at her, I felt a wave of power wash through me, aimed straight at Miss Chutney. I jerked my hand aside at the last instant. The ground by her feet exploded in a shower of soil. I clenched my fists, afraid of what I might do.

"Look what you did to me," I said, holding up my wrist, still covered with red marks and scratches from the bracelet.

"No, oh, dear no. I came to help you. I was sure that—"

"Stop. I'm not listening to you. Stay away from me. Just stay away. I'm warning you. You can't have my power." I felt weak. The blast must have drained a lot out of me. I didn't think I could cast another spell.

She started to rub her hands together. I ran back inside. Maybe her spells wouldn't work if I got out of her sight.

I didn't really feel safe until I got to history. At least Elestra was watching out for me. When she handed out our study sheets, she paused at my desk and smiled at me.

I walked home by myself. Jan had to stay for a meeting of the school paper. Halfway home, I heard footsteps rushing up from behind me.

It was Miss Chutney again. She grabbed at my backpack.

"Stay away from me," I warned her, pulling free from her grasp. "Just stay away."

"But, dear—" She rubbed her hands together.

"Leave me alone." I ran down the street, but it was too late—she'd launched another attack. I heard a tearing sound behind me. It took me a second to realize where it was coming from. My backpack! Something was alive in there. Every day, I slipped the backpack on and off without trouble. Now, I struggled to get it off. One strap caught at my elbow. My terror grew as a claw burst through the fabric right next to my back.

"No!" I gasped as I tugged at the strap. The claw slashed at me, slicing through my shirt as if it were made of cobwebs.

I yanked the backpack from my arm and flung it into the street just as a school bus came by. The front tire crushed the pack. Then the rear tire sent the pack tumbling along the road.

I waited. Nothing happened. I walked over and picked up the pack. White dust dribbled from a rip. My books and papers were scattered all over. I looked behind me. Miss Chutney was where I had left her, a block away. "It didn't work!" I shouted. "You didn't get me." I jammed everything I could find back into the pack, then rushed off.

Darling was waiting for me in my room. "I am so glad to be home," I said, rubbing my hand along her wonderfully soft back.

"Mewrlll," she said.

I plunked down on my bed and looked at my backpack. Nothing much was damaged, except for the pack itself where it had been ripped. The shirt was probably ruined—it had long slashes in the back. My books were okay, but I couldn't find my history study sheet. At least the test wasn't until next week.

I sat and did my homework. As I was finishing up, I heard little footsteps scuffing along the hallway.

"Angelina, look what I got," Rory said, holding up a comic book with a picture of wizards and dragons on the cover.

"Great," I said. "Where'd you get it?"

"This nice old lady gave it to me."

Nice old lady? I had to get it away from him. "Rory, can I borrow it?"

"Sure. I like to share with you."

"Thanks." I put the comic book in my closet after Rory left my room. As I walked back from the closet, I glanced at my bookshelf. I realized I'd never found out what *dispatch* meant. My heart slammed against my chest when I read the definition in the dictionary. *Dispatch* could mean a letter, or it could mean *to send something*. But it also meant *to destroy*.

He who seeks to steal power must dispatch the holder.

Twenty-five

OUT ON THE TOWN

I ran to Jan's house. "I'm not keeping the power," I told her when she answered the door. "I'll spend the rest of my life looking over my shoulder. Anyone can steal my power if they kill me." I wondered how many people out there were searching for power. There could be hundreds of them heading to Lewington at this moment, like bloodhounds sniffing out a hidden steak.

Jan shuddered. She looked past me toward the street. "Come on inside."

We went up to her room. "Can't you protect yourself with your power?" Jan asked.

I shook my head. "I'm not living my life behind walls—even if they're magical or invisible walls. Tomorrow—somehow—I'm passing my power along to its rightful owner."

"Tomorrow?" Jan asked.

I told her what the book said. "Power is freely given on the fifth day of possession. This must be done in a place of power, at a time of power, before five minutes have flown."

"So where's that?" Jan asked.

"I don't know where. But I know tomorrow is the right day. Look." I went over to the calendar she had on the wall next to her bed. "Saturday, it happened in the park. That's the first day. Then Sunday, Monday, Tuesday. So Wednesday is the fifth day." As my finger traced the days, I saw what Jan had written on the calendar. "Wait! Of course . . ."

"Angie, what is it?"

"My place of power. It's so obvious. Everything is connected with the number five. Five days, five minutes. My place of power is—"

"The mall!" Jan said.

"Right. And the time has to be midnight. The very start of the day. The witching hour." I looked at Jan's clock. It was four thirty. I just had to stay alive for seven and a half hours and make sure I was at the mall before midnight.

"Why can't the world be nicer?" Jan asked. "Why can't everyone leave you alone and let you do some good with your power?"

"It's not the way things work," I said. "But it can be! For just a little while. I might not have power tomorrow, but I have it now." I grabbed Jan's hand. "Come on— let's do some good."

"Where?" she asked as she let me drag her down the steps.

"I don't know." I went into the street and looked around. The first thing I saw was Mrs. Grunwald's roof across the street. It was old and leaky, and I'd heard Mom say that Mrs. Grunwald couldn't afford to get it fixed right now. So I fixed it, making sure it would never leak again. And it felt good. I ran up the street, doing small favors for my neighbors. Mr. Carmichael's garage door would never get stuck again, and Ms. Lalbie's car would always start, no matter how cold it got in the morning.

As I told Jan what I was doing, she got right into the spirit of it, cheering me on and suggesting things for me to do. When we'd covered the neighborhood, we went toward town.

"Where could we do the most good?" I asked Jan.

"The food bank?" she suggested.

"Good idea." There was a building at the edge of downtown where they gave meals to anyone who was hungry. When we got there, I stopped and looked in the front window. I could see a small kitchen inside.

"Here goes," I said. I took a deep breath and cast my spell. A big box filled with cans of food and packages of pasta appeared in the corner. Nobody noticed it right away. That was good. When they found it, they'd figure somebody left it there for them.

Once we got started, it was hard to stop. The senior citizens' home got a new coat of paint, the hospital got a

128

bunch of great books for the kids' section, and I got rid of all the rust on the playground equipment at the elementary school.

"Well, the world's a little bit of a better place," Jan said, pausing to catch her breath. She'd been running to keep up with me.

"The world's better," I said, "but I feel like a bowl of overcooked spaghetti."

Jan made a face. "That doesn't sound very tasty. I feel like a hot-fudge sundae."

I shook my head. "No. I mean that's how I *feel*. I'm wiped out. I'd better get some rest before tonight. Do you mind?"

"Not at all," Jan said.

I was going to apologize for not doing any fun things, but I realized it wasn't true. We'd had a great time.

Jan walked me home, then said, "I'll meet you at the mall."

"See you there." I went up to my room, set the alarm for eleven fifteen, and collapsed on the bed.

Soon after I woke, there was a light tap at my door. "Come in," I said.

Rory walked in, holding the bird that Dad had sent him.

"Can't sleep?" I asked.

He shook his head. Then he looked around the room like he wanted to ask me something but didn't know how to begin. "What is it?" I asked him.

"Can you make me fly?"

"What?" I asked.

"You can do stuff. Can't you? Like with Sebastian?"

"So you saw what I did?" I'd figured he hadn't noticed.

Rory shrugged. "I'm just little. Not stupid."

Wow—he was right. I was so used to thinking of him as this little kid who didn't really understand what was going on. "Sorry. I know what you mean. I'll give it a try." I took the plastic bird and lifted it in my hand. *Fly,* I thought. *Please fly, Rory.* I imagined harder than I'd ever imagined anything. I gave it all my concentration.

"Yay," Rory said as he rose. He flew. Actually, it was more like he was swimming in the air, but he loved it. I tried to keep the spell going, but after five minutes, he sank gently back to the floor. I guess I was still pretty tired out.

"That's it?" Rory asked.

"Yeah. Sorry it wasn't longer."

"That's okay. It was great! Thanks!" He gave me a hug, then walked out the door and back to his room. He was really an awesome kid. I realized I was still holding the bird. I tossed it on my bed.

I looked at the clock. It was eleven thirty—time to go to my place of power. There was only one question: Was the rightful owner waiting there for me?

I was just about to leave the room when my closet door burst open and my bedroom door slammed shut.

130

Twenty-six

FLIGHT

Long green vines with sharp thorns snaked out from the closet. They flowed from the comic book, like lava from a volcano. In seconds, the vines had blocked the door to the hallway.

"Stop!" I shouted, trying to focus my concentration on holding the vines back.

They kept coming.

Darling hissed. I stooped and grabbed her. By the time I'd put her out of danger on my dresser, the vines had reached me. Two of them wrapped around my ankles. They were stronger than I expected. I was yanked off my feet.

The vines dragged me toward the closet where, at the center of this nightmare plant, leaves with knifelike jagged tips slashed and stabbed the air.

As I was dragged past my bed, I saw Rory's toy bird.

I grabbed it and wound it up, then held it so the wings flapped toward the vines. With the aid of my power, I amplified the breeze, turning it into a blast of wind that pushed against the vines. The force ripped leaves right off the vines. Slowly, their grip on my legs loosened. The wings stopped flapping after a moment, but that didn't matter. Once I'd started the blast, I could keep it going.

The vines, pushed flat against the walls around the closet, were starting to wilt. I'd won, but I'd used up much of my strength.

"What's all that noise?" Mom called from down the hallway.

I inched toward my door and opened it. Sebastian was looking out from his room. "I have to go somewhere," I told him.

"No problem," he said. "I'll cover for you."

"Really?"

He grinned. "Sure. Don't worry. Go do what you have to do. And be careful. Okay?"

"Okay."

He headed down the hall toward Mom's room. I heard him say, "Sorry about the noise, Mom. I was try-ing to pick up the mess in my room."

"At eleven thirty at night?" Mom asked.

"Gee, is it that late? Sorry. I'll try to be more quiet. I wouldn't want to wake Angie."

I looked back at the vines. They'd all fallen into dust. I had to get to the mall. I didn't want to risk getting caught by going down the hallway. The window was my best chance. The porch roof was right below my room. I put Darling outside, then stepped through to join her. I hung by my hands and dropped to the lawn.

"Come on, jump!" I called to Darling, holding out my hands. She was part of this, and I knew I had to take her with me.

She stood for a moment at the edge, then leaped into my arms. I heard footsteps to my left. Miss Chutney was running out from a car parked up the street.

There were other steps. I looked to my right. Elestra was running toward me from that side. "Wait," she cried.

"No time," I called. I ran all the way to the park, right past the bench where it had all started. This had been the old lady's place of power, with the five trees circling the bench. But it wasn't my place of power. That lay at the end of the path.

A huge sign above the entrance blazed ahead of me: MIDNIGHT MADNESS SALE.

I ran in through Main Mall past the bank. The clock flashed the time and temperature. It was seventy-three degrees. It was 11:55.

The mall was mobbed. People were dashing all around, going crazy over the sales. There were decorations everywhere. Streamers hung from the walls, and balloons were tied to almost every available place. I pushed through the crowds, cradling Darling to protect her, and wondered whether I had made a mistake. As the sign had said, this seemed more a place of madness than of power. But if this was my place of power, I needed to get near the center. I raced onto the footbridge, then stopped with a sickening jolt. I couldn't cross the running water.

I looked around. Elestra was coming in through the Main Mall entrance. I looked toward North Mall. Miss Chutney was huffing down the corridor toward me, rubbing her hands together. Elestra spotted me. She waved her arms and shouted something.

Then I heard another shout.

"Angie!"

I looked behind me. Jan stood at the entrance to South Mall. A crowd milled around the Hub, but it seemed as if they'd all faded to gray while Jan stood out in color. I sensed that there was even more going on. I looked toward East Mall. Again, one person stood out from the crowd. May Mellon waited there, at the edge of the corridor, staring at me.

And in the West? I knew even before I looked. Katrina walked slowly toward me, but stared down at the ground.

Power seeks its rightful owner.

I checked the clock. 11:58.

At the entrance to North Mall, Miss Chutney shouted and rubbed her hands together.

Something rustled at my feet. It was a sales slip someone had dropped. The small piece of paper started to change shape, growing round and slender and alive. Before my eyes, it became a snake.

135

I'd spent so much time when I was younger reading about Cleopatra that I instantly recognized the snake. It was an asp. It was deadly. Someone was trying to dispatch me.

Twenty-seven

FIGHT

I tried to step away from the asp but was blocked by the flowing water. I started to stumble. My hands fell open. Darling leaped from me and grabbed the snake by the neck. She shook it with a sharp jerk of her head, snapping it like a rope. It turned to dust between her teeth. She didn't seem too happy about the dust part.

I looked at each of the five people surrounding me. Everyone else in the mall faded like ghosts. I stood at the center of this five-armed place of power, knowing it was time to keep my gift or pass it along.

"Your father is in danger," Elestra said. "Give me the power. I can save him. Look, and you'll see the danger is real. Use your vision." She pointed toward the ceiling.

As I stared into the dome over my head, the glass filled with the scene of a car—Dad's car—approaching a train crossing. Classical music blared from the stereo.

I knew Dad used it to help keep awake when he was tired. It was so loud, he'd never hear the train.

There was a dreadful crash as the train struck the side of the car. I closed my eyes. When I opened them, the image was gone.

"How?" I asked. "How do I give the power to you?"

"Just touch me and let it flow," she said. She walked toward the edge of the bridge. "Hurry. There isn't much time."

She was right—there wasn't much time. But there was enough time to wonder about one thing. She was so lovely and so kind, so helpful, so easy to trust. Too easy to trust. "No, not that way," I said. I pointed toward the other side of the bridge. "Come around."

She looked at the running water, then glared at me. That's when I knew. "You already have power," I said. "Admit it."

Elestra shook her head. "Not enough. Not nearly enough. What good is it? All I can cast are small spells with paper. Nothing lasts. It all turns so easily to dust. I need more. Then the world will be mine." She stopped.

I could tell from her face that she realized she'd said too much. *Spells with paper.* All the things that had attacked me—they began as paper. The money, the bracelet, the history study sheet, the comic book—all paper. And all Elestra's doing. I'd been fooled by her beauty. I almost smiled as I remembered Rory's words. He'd told me an old lady had given him the comic book. To a really young kid like him, I guess she looked like an old lady.

"Give me your power," she said, stepping up on the bridge. "Give it and I'll save your father. Make me take it and I'll do nothing for him."

"Don't trust her!"

I turned toward my left. Miss Chutney was waving her arms for my attention and shouting. "She uses her power for evil!"

I looked at Elestra. She'd done nothing but lie. Maybe she'd lied when she said I couldn't save my father.

"You're wasting time," Elestra said, taking a step toward me.

I knew I could save him. But how? I was best with air. I grabbed a balloon from the railing of the bridge and squeezed it. At this point, I felt that I had almost nothing left inside me. But I put all my thought and effort into the air in his left front tire. Slowly, I felt the balloon, and the tire, expanding, swelling, bulging.

The balloon burst in my hands. The pressure in my mind vanished. I'd done all I could. I looked at the clock. It was three minutes after twelve. I dropped to one knee, exhausted by the effort of that spell.

"Give me your power now, or I will take it." Elestra spread her arms. Around me, dozens of slips of paper began to shiver and swell and change. "Do what I say."

I shook my head. "No way."

Elestra got an odd look on her face and staggered back a step. I'd done something to her, but I didn't know what. It couldn't have been a spell—I didn't have the energy left for anything powerful.

"It has to be," Elestra said.

"Stay away from me," I warned.

Elestra screamed and took another step backwards.

I heard Jan shout from behind me, "It rhymed! Angie, do it again."

Rhymed? Jan was right. Elestra had said, *It has to be.* Then I'd said, *Stay away from me.* That must be the way I could fight her power. I just had to keep making rhymes. That wouldn't be hard. Even I could find rhymes for *be* and *me.*

Before I could think of anything, Elestra shouted, "*Silver! Orange!*"

I stood, my mouth open, not knowing what to say. Nothing rhymed with either of those words. Elestra spoke them over and over as she waved her arms and spun in dizzying circles, pouring all her power into one deadly spell.

At my feet, creatures born of discarded paper crawled, hissing and snarling, toward me. From the water below, lizards with fangs and worms with claws slithered up the sides of the bridge. All around the mall, signs and posters started to transform. To my right, in the bookstore, a hundred thousand creatures descended from the shelves. To my left, greeting cards flapped and flew like bats from the display racks.

Every piece of paper in the mall was coming to kill me.

"Now you'll be destroyed!" Elestra screamed. "And after you, all your friends. Silver, orange! Silver, orange!"

Twenty-eight

DECISION

I should have been paralyzed with fear. The Angelina of five days ago might have been. I'd grown up a little since then. My mind, faced with so much hate and greed, grew calm. In that instant, the answer came to me. Backwards. I reversed her words, saying them backwards. There was power in reversal. "Egnaro, revlis!" I shouted. All I needed was a rhyme. *Egnaro* rhymed with *tomorrow*. And *revlis* was easy. I had it.

"Now, not tomorrow, just end this." I pointed at her and shouted again, "End this!" I gave the shout all my strength and power. Then I fell to my knees.

Wind swept past me, lifting the paper-born creatures, sweeping them off in a flutter of slashing claws and snapping fangs. Their howls and shrieks faded as they turned to dust. The wind grew stronger, forcing me flat on my stomach. Elestra shot backwards as if yanked by a giant rubber band. She flew down the corridor of Main Mall, propelled by the force of her own power turned against her, and disappeared out the door.

I got to my feet, turned slowly, and looked at the others. They still stood apart from the crowds in the mall. It was four minutes after twelve. If I was to give away the power, it had to be now.

I looked at Miss Chutney. "You want the power, don't you?"

She smiled sadly. "I want it too much." She shook her head and rubbed her hands together. I realized it was a nervous habit, and nothing more. "I would be a bad choice."

I understood what she meant. She'd chased the power all her life but wasn't meant to have it. But that didn't solve my problem. "I don't know what to do," I said.

"Keep it," Miss Chutney said. "Keep the power."

A fly buzzed past my head and landed on the railing. It took off and buzzed past me again. Annoyed, I waved it away with my hand. It fell dead to the ground.

I looked at the body of the fly and thought about what I had done in the last five days. I'd played pranks. I'd broken pencils. I'd done some good, but no more than I could have done with a bit of hard work. Would I help people, or would I end up hurting them?

I shook my head. "I would be a bad choice, too."

I turned toward the others. Katrina still stood there, not saying a word. May glared at me, full of anger. "Katrina?" I said.

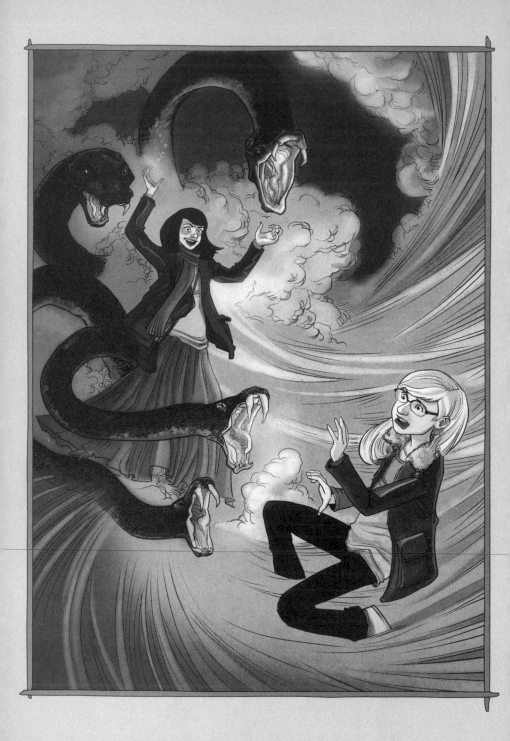

She looked up at me. I understood what had happened. She'd been following me, hoping to get to know me, but too shy to speak up—so shy, she'd fled to the park when I said hi to her. She wasn't looking for power; she was looking for a friend. I'd probably be a bad choice for that, too. We had nothing in common.

"Katrina, this is May," I said. "May, this is Katrina. I think you two might like each other if you spent some time together."

They looked at each other. I watched them. May, full of anger and desperate for acceptance. Katrina, painfully shy and afraid of everything. Maybe I was wrong, but I suspected that they could do more for each other than any power I could give them. I dug deep for a spark of power and cast a spell—it wasn't strong, and I didn't even know if it worked, but I did my best to make them great friends. I blew them a kiss to seal the magic.

Then I turned toward Jan.

"Don't even think about it," she warned. "I don't want your power."

"Yeah," I agreed. "It's too much." I paused, took a deep breath, and cast my final spell. It was very small, but it was important. I glanced down at my feet to make sure it had worked.

"So who gets it?" Jan asked.

"You do," I said.

"No!" Jan shouted.

I smiled. "But not just you. Everyone gets to share." I raised my arms and pointed both hands at the domed

145

ceiling of the mall. "Go," I whispered. As I set it free, the power within me that had been drained and dulled from the spells I'd cast returned in full force. Power flowed from me like water, and like fire and earth and air. It surged toward the sky and struck the dome, then splashed outward, washing the mall and everyone inside with its magic glow.

I kept my eyes on the dome. In the image on the ceiling, a car skidded to the shoulder of the road. I saw Dad step out of the car and look at the tire. Down the road from him, a train roared through an unlit crossing.

As the last of the power left me, the crowds throughout the mall came back into focus. All around, people started to laugh and smile.

"I found a dollar," a woman said. "This is my lucky day."

"That's it!" a man shouted. "I know how to fix that problem at work."

A young girl started singing in a lovely voice. A man danced past me as if he'd just discovered his gift.

Everyone looked happy and alive and touched with just a bit of power.

I glanced at Katrina and May. They were talking. Well, actually, May was talking and Katrina was listening. I looked at Miss Chutney. She smiled sadly. "Come visit me, girls."

"We will," Jan said.

"Mewrl." Darling brushed against my leg.

I picked her up in one hand, grabbed the bag that

was at my feet with the other hand, and walked down the bridge over the running stream. "Here," I said, handing Jan the bag.

She took it and looked inside. "Hot-fudge sundaes! You remembered." She looked up and asked, "Extra fudge?"

"Absolutely." We walked toward the exit.

"Triple scoop?"

"Yup." We went out the door.

"Two cherries?"

"Sure thing." I looked back at the sign and smiled.

"Nuts?"

"Certainly." The sign now said: MIDNIGHT MAGIC SALE.

"No calories?"

"Jan," I said, putting my arm around my best friend, "that wouldn't be magic. That would be a miracle."

Twenty-nine

BACK HOME

I guess my life is back to normal. Dad got home late and dirty from changing his flat tire. He told us he saw a train cross the road at a spot where the signal wasn't working. I just hugged him and didn't say anything. He was so happy to be safe that he didn't mind at all about Darling.

Rory keeps talking about this great dream he had one night where he flew around the house. He always grins at me after he tells the story. Rory got hugs, too.

Sebastian is as obnoxious as always. I thanked him for helping me, but somehow we ended up fighting a few minutes later. He started it, of course. I didn't hug him. Then again, I can't turn him into a lizard or a pile of slime or anything cool, so I guess he shouldn't complain.

Katrina and May became best friends. They even

dress alike. One day, they wear plain skirts and blue shirts; the next, they wear these wonderfully hideous tropical patterns. The kids in school don't understand this friendship, and still make fun of them. Of course, they only make fun of May behind her back. Actually, they're careful around Katrina, too, these days. Maybe they can't understand what those two have found in each other, but I can.

Jan and I visit Miss Chutney all the time. She's a wonderful lady and knows a lot of interesting stuff, like how to remove a love spell. That came in handy with Clem and Clyde. I have a feeling that if I hadn't done something, they would have ended up beating each other senseless.

As for me—I'm just a normal girl again. That's fine. I like my life. It seems that everyone in the mall got a tiny bit of power, and there are now lots of people in Lewington who can do things they couldn't do before. I've started writing poetry. I seem to have developed a gift for it. Miss Chutney has started doing card tricks, of all things. Jan claims she isn't sure what her bit of magic is, but I think she's keeping it a secret from me. I'm sure she'll tell me sooner or later.

Believe it or not, even the mall got some of the power. But that's another story.

Kids can be such monsters . . . literally!
Especially at Washington Irving Elementary. Read on for a sneak peek at
The Wavering Werewolf. . . .

A small creature dashed across the path, skittering out of the woods on one side of the trail, then back in on the other side. I caught just enough of a glimpse to know it was a rabbit. I stepped to the edge of the path and stared at the spot where the animal had run.

That's when I heard the growl.

Actually, it was more of a snarl. Well, it was sort of a half snarl–half growl sound. The differences probably weren't important at the moment. The key feature here was the threatening nature of the sound. This was not some form of animal greeting or mating call. This sounded more like "Hello, lunch."

I took off, picking the more active half of the fight-or-flight reaction, and stumbled from the path into the woods. Some small part of my mind was amused that I seemed to be choosing the same route as the rabbit.

The rest of my mind was busy urging my body to move faster. Running is not my best activity, but I must say I achieved a new personal record as I tore through the underbrush.

Unfortunately, whatever was chasing me had a lot more experience in this version of tag. The growling sounds got closer. They were right behind me. Then they were right on me. Something slammed into my back.

I fell face-forward. The force made me roll right over. It was the first time in my life I had ever done a somersault. I didn't like it. As I slammed to a stop, my glasses bounced from my head. I panicked at the thought of losing them, but I got lucky. When I groped through the leaves that surrounded me, I felt the frames right away.

Before I could put on my glasses or stand up, something gray and sleek and fast landed on my chest. It was so close to me that it was mostly a blur, but it was a blur with a mouth and a tongue and teeth—especially teeth. Even without my glasses, I could tell that the blurry teeth ended in blurry points of the kind designed to make holes in just about anything. The teeth appeared about ready to bite my face. This wasn't a good thing.

I raised my hand as the animal lunged closer, the mouth so wide, it looked like my whole head would disappear inside. A wave of hot, raw animal breath washed over me.

About the Author

David Lubar grew up in Morristown, New Jersey. His books include *Hidden Talents*, an ALA Best Book for Young Adults; *True Talents*; *Flip*, a VOYA Best Science Fiction, Fantasy, and Horror selection; the Weenies short-story collections *In the Land of the Lawn Weenies*, *Invasion of the Road Weenies*, *The Curse of the Campfire Weenies*, *The Battle of the Red Hot Pepper Weenies*, *Attack of the Vampire Weenies*, and *Beware the Ninja Weenies*; and the Nathan Abercrombie, Accidental Zombie series. He lives in Nazareth, Pennsylvania. You can visit him on the Web at www.davidlubar.com.